# The Vengeance
# of Amelia Earhart

## And Other Tales

By Matt Snee

*For my parents,*

*Ron and Joyce*

# Table of Contents

# The Vengeance of Amelia Earhart

<u>**1.**</u>

They met in a café, of course, in Paris, in 1932. Simone was drinking her tea when a tall woman wearing pants and sporting brash short hair approached her, asking if she could spare a cigarette.

"Of course," said Simone, digging into her pockets. The woman's accent was terrible. Simone knew immediately she was an American.

"Thank you," said the woman. Simone could sense she had less interest in the cigarette and more in making a friend.

"What's your name, dear?"

"Simone de Beauvoir," Simone replied.

"Ah," said the woman. "I am Amelia. Amelia Earhart."

The name sounded familiar to Simone.

"What do you do for a living?" Amelia asked.

"I'm a teacher," said Simone.

"What do you teach?"

"Whatever I can," Simone laughed, "but mostly secondary education."

"Ah," said Amelia, chuckling to herself in a manly sort of way.

"And you?"

"I'm… I guess you would consider me somewhat of a celebrity now," said Amelia. "Despite myself. I'm an aviator, from America." Amelia's voice was full of cautious pride.

"An aviator? An airplane pilot?" Simone was impressed.

"Yes."

Simone now gave Amelia all of her attention. A female aviator!

"I am American," Amelia admitted. "I hope you don't fault me."

"Not at all!" said Simone.

"I just flew over the Atlantic a month ago."

"Like Lindberg!"

"Yes, I suppose. Unfortunately, while I planned to land in Paris, I ended up in a pasture in Ireland." Amelia laughed slightly.

"Well, I confuse Parisians with cows all the time!" joked Simone.

Amelia smiled, one corner of her mouth curled higher than the other.

It was the beginning of a strange friendship.

*

Simone returned home to the flat she shared with Jean-Paul Sartre. She was aglow.

"What is it?" Sartre asked her.

"I met someone truly interesting today," she confessed. "A female aviator. From America."

"Is she beautiful?" Sartre asked.

"Yes," Simone answered.

They were both young. Sartre was twenty-seven and Simone was only twenty-four. They each taught outside the city for most of the year but enjoyed a two-week holiday in Paris every summer. They imagined themselves to be young geniuses who were destined for greatness.

"She's invited us to a club, tomorrow night," said Simone.

"Women of your persuasion can certainly sense their kind," said Sartre.

"I told her I'd bring you too."

"And?"

"She didn't seem to mind."

"Ah. A true libertine. I'm impossibly intrigued." A sly smile danced on his lips.

Sartre went back to his book, and Simone tried her best to read as well, but the presence of Amelia lingered in her mind. She had been impressed by the woman — a female celebrity, famous for her achievements, not her beauty.

It was everything Simone wanted for her own future.

*

The next night Sartre and Simone arrived at the club dressed smartly. Sartre raised his eyebrow like an out of place comma as he held the door to the club for Simone.

"This place – on our salaries?"

"Don't be a grump," Simone scolded. "We are here as Amelia's guests. She said she'd pay."

"Is she an heiress?" He asked.

"Better… she's a star," replied Simone.

Inside, Parisians danced and dined to American big band music. A blond haired German singer belted standards while wiggling her hips. It was both wondrous and appalling.

Simone and Sartre found Amelia inside, situated at the back of the club, in a VIP section. She sat at a large, round booth and got up as soon as she saw Simone approach, kissing her familiarly on the cheek. She shook Sartre's hand firmly and welcomed them both.

"Hello, my friends!" Amelia spoke loudly over the music.

They sat, pushing themselves into the swallowing fabric of the booth. Amelia positioned herself in between Simone and Sartre. When the waitress came over, Amelia delicately placed her hand on Simone's thigh and asked what she would like to drink.

"American whiskey!" Simone laughed at Amelia's boldness.

"One whiskey," Amelia repeated to the waitress. "And you, Jean-Paul?"

"The same."

"Make that two whiskeys!" Amelia told the waitress. "And another water for me!"

When the waitress departed, Sartre asked Amelia why she had ordered water.

"I don't drink," she replied. "I prefer to live life in desperate sober determination."

Sartre laughed, and Simone joined him.

"Are you a real Grecian heroine?" Sartre asked her.

"I am," Amelia replied.

The waitress returned with their drinks. Simone sipped hers quickly to cover her nervousness. Once those drinks were finished, more were ordered.

And more after that.

*

Simone, after having too many whiskeys, invited Amelia back to their flat, to listen to some music on their newly purchased gramophone. Amelia hastily agreed. As they walked down the Parisian streets, Amelia slipped between Simone and Sartre, interlacing her arms with theirs.

Soon enough the trio climbed the steps to Simone and Sartre's holiday flat, and Sartre unlocked the door. Inside, Sartre took Amelia's coat, and the aviator flopped down on the couch, crossing her legs and lighting a cigarette. She was wearing custom fit trousers. Despite their masculine silhouette, they strangely accented her female form.

Simone itched in her dress. Feeling the fabric cinch in at her waist and across her thighs, she pulled it up slightly to release some of the tension. Drunk and somewhat bold from the whiskey, she sat next to Amelia and laid her head on Amelia's shoulder. In response, Amelia leaned into Simone and placed her hand on Simone's bare thigh.

Sartre unscrewed some wine and drank directly from the bottle, before lighting a cigarette and putting jazz on the record player. He excused himself to go to the toilet.

Amelia whispered softly into Simone's ear. Simone didn't catch what was said. The music played. Sartre returned from the bathroom without his pants, revealing his blue underwear, and black socks pulled up to his knees.

Both women laughed.

"You seem to have forgotten your trousers, my love," said Simone.

"I have not forgotten them, I have forgotten where I put them," he argued.

Simone stretched out her hand towards Sartre in noble gesture. "Amelia, his Highness the Great Philosopher."

"Ha, ha, ha," he snickered at Simone. He said softly to Amelia, "She thinks up all of my better ideas."

Simone rolled her eyes.

Sartre fell into the couch next to Amelia. "So. Are you going to put your hand on my thigh too?" he asked.

Amelia smiled her crooked smile and laid her hand on his hairy leg. Sartre winked at Simone and leaned in to kiss Amelia. Amelia kissed back. Amelia turned her head to Simone and kissed her gently on the lips. The aviator's lips were warm and soft.

Once they made their way into the bedroom, their clothes came off without trepidation. They laughed as though they had discovered something new. Simone had little interest in Sartre and Sartre had little interest in Simone. They both competed for the affections of Amelia.

Sartre won. He rolled Amelia over onto her stomach and smirked at Simone, who reclined and took a cigarette from a case. She watched them for a while, until bored, she stepped half-naked out of the room and went to the kitchen where she had bread and jam. She drank a glass of cold water, which was delightful on her parched throat after a night of drinking.

Simone ate by herself in the moonlit kitchen. The jam left a sticky residue on her fingers and lips. Once finished, she lit another cigarette and exhaled gray smoke up into the ceiling fan.

Amelia came out of the bedroom, stark naked, and found Simone washing her dish in the basin. The legendary aviator pressed her body against Simone's back, and Simone could feel Amelia's breasts against her skin.

"Just having a snack," said Simone, a little nervous.

"Me too," said Amelia.

They kissed. Simone turned, and Amelia cupped her buttocks gently.

"Come to the couch with me," Amelia cooed.

Simone did not hesitate.

*

Once sated, they talked.

Amelia spoke of her life back home. Amelia had a husband whom she respected, but admitted her fame had caused a small wedge between them. This cold dose of reality hit Simone and left her chilled. She raised herself to her feet and started a fire in the fireplace to bring some warmth back into the room. When she turned back from the hearth, she found Amelia fast asleep on the sofa.

Simone covered Amelia with a blanket from the back of the couch and went into the bedroom, where she found Sartre lying on his back. His head was turned as he watched the sunrise through the window.

"So, what do you think?" Simone asked.

"I think contrary to criticism, she is definitely a woman," he laughed.

Simone lit a cigarette. "I had a nice evening."

"It was ok," said Sartre.

Simone finished the cigarette and crawled in bed beside Sartre. She laid her head on his chest.

"I'm tired," she whispered, drifting off to sleep.

It was late morning when she awoke, and Simone found herself alone in the bed. She threw her robe on and went into the other room. Sartre and Amelia sat at the kitchen table dining on a fresh baguette Sartre had fetched from the market, along with sardines.

Simone joined them and ate again, astonished at her hunger.

Shortly before noon, Amelia dressed and apologized that she must go. None of them suggested meeting again.

After Amelia politely pecked Sartre on the cheek, she kissed Simone deeply.

"I'll see you again," she said.

<u>**2.**</u>

They didn't see each other again until the winter of 1934, when Amelia came to spend a week with Simone and Sartre at their home in Le Havre. On the second day of the visit, Simone and Amelia walked along a snow-covered beach beside the English Channel. Their hands warmed in their pockets beneath a cloudy sky. An incorrigible wind tossed snow and sand into their coats and twirled their hair.

"I like it here," said Amelia. "I like things that are cold, miserable, and beautiful."

"Then it's no wonder you like me," joked Simone.

Amelia laughed. "You are neither cold nor miserable, my dear."

"I can be both when I am displeased," Simone assured her.

They stepped across the beach, watching the sea.

"I wish I were a kite, on windy days like this," said Amelia. "Hovering in the air, flapping back and forth. I'd snap my string, and just… go."

"You are always thinking of flying!" giggled Simone.

"I suppose," said Amelia. "I suppose I am," she repeated. "I could take you flying while I'm here…"

"Maybe next time," said Simone, declining one thing and promising another.

The air got colder as the day went on, and they hurried back to the warmth of the house. Sartre was cooking lunch and filling the house with the delicious odor of roasted chicken. They sat and dined. Simone and Sartre shared a bottle of chardonnay while Amelia sipped coffee. Their silverware clinked across the plates as they told jokes.

Simone told Sartre that back in the States, Amelia had a clothing line named after her and that she appeared in advertisements.

"Really?" asked Sartre. "You're becoming an institution, my dear."

"I do what my husband tells me, sometimes," she mused.

Simone groaned. "A ghastly arrangement, if you ask me."

"Putnam is a good man," Amelia argued. "Funny sometimes. And good with money."

"We're both terrible with money, aren't we, my dear?" Sartre asked Simone.

"Dreadful with it," agreed Simone.

"I grew up with it, and then lost it," said Amelia. "I appreciate it more now."

"Oh, we appreciate it," said Sartre. "So much that we spend it all." He gestured to the stacks of books upon the floor.

"Our fortune," he told her.

*

While Sartre slept, Simone and Amelia talked late into the night again. Simone described the books she wanted to write, and Amelia gushed about her plans to be the first woman to fly around the entire world. These talks were interspersed with lovemaking. Simone found Amelia to be somewhat insatiable. She kept up with the aviator as best she could.

On her last night, Amelia told Simone more about her home in New York.

"You would love it," said Amelia. "Planks of gold light come through the windows, and fresh air comes off the meadows, the tall trees, the blue river. It's so quiet sometimes I believe the whole world has stopped turning."

"Sounds beautiful," said Simone.

"You should come to visit," offered Amelia. "I can show you America."

"Only if you fly me there," Simone teased.

"I will!" Amelia promised. "God," she breathed. "I think I love you."

"Oh," said Simone. "Don't bring up love, never love. That's for emasculated men and frail-hearted school girls…"

"You are always the scholar," Amelia countered. "What word should I use?"

"Tell me you adore me, that is enough."

"Then I adore you, Simone. I adore you more than the sky adores the moon!"

The next day, Amelia left, wiping tears from her eyes. Simone was sad to see her go. Sartre embraced the aviator and told her she was always welcome; however, it was apparent he was tired of their guest.

Simone and Sartre watched Amelia's car depart down the road. Sartre eagerly went inside to finish his breakfast. Simone waited until the car was completely out of her sight.

*

Despite their professions, both Simone and Sartre believed true wisdom was earned, not learned; the result of a mixture of life experience, hardship, and accomplishment. Freedom wasn't the result of how much money you had in your pocket, or if you had a gun in your hand; it could only be found in your heart.

Simone and Sartre were writing as much as they were reading. Dreams of intellectual grandeur filled their minds. Their shared passion brought them closer than ever as they sat at opposite ends of the house, working in their off hours. They both were atheists and believed the meaning in life must be forged by ourselves. As their intellectual paths united them, their single-minded devotions to their art caused a divide.

When Amelia returned in the summer of 1935, Simone and Sartre still lived in Le Havre but had taken separate living quarters, no longer sharing their household. Their bond remained strong, but they found living apart gave them the space to work harder on their philosophical endeavors.

Simone had a flat overlooking the port. Amelia visited her there. The two of them would watch the ships come in as they sat in various stages of undress between bouts of love and discussion. Simone noticed during this visit, Amelia was disinterested in spending as much time with Sartre. Simone secretly enjoyed the extra attention from the aviator, who had arrived brandishing new accomplishments, accolades… and money.

The ladies would dine out in the finest establishments in the city and casually walk back in the summer breeze, linking arms, hesitant to sever the connection. Amelia always wore trousers, claiming the last time she wore a skirt was when she met

U.S. President Calvin Coolidge, back in '32. Simone enjoyed beautiful dresses and shoes.

Even though there seemed to be a mismatch to this perversely bourgeois detail, they were on equal footing in their relationship. Simone adored and respected Amelia; she wanted to live like her. While Amelia was possessive at times, Simone thought nothing of it.

When the three of them reunited for an evening at Sartre's house, it was fun and carefree; however, Simone noticed something about Amelia had innately changed. Amelia was less forgiving of Sartre's idiosyncrasies and male buffooneries; at the same time, Sartre seemed tired of the American. Simone forgave Sartre his short temper and contributed it to the passion he had for his latest work, which was consuming him.

When the night was over, Sartre kissed Simone but shook Amelia's hand before closing the door quickly behind them. They took a cab back to Simone's flat. The mood of the evening had left Simone feeling uneasy. Amelia wanted to make love, but Simone noticed a quiet disconnect.

At the end of Amelia's trip, she once again asked Simone if she would visit her in the States, promising her to fly her in her airplane one way or another.

"I'd love to," said Simone, "But I'm so busy with work at the moment. I'm working on a terrible novel, and school has me up to my ears. But, my dear, maybe next year, we'll see."

Simone had little intention of actually visiting Amelia – the trip over the ocean was too daunting. Besides, why did she need to go, when Amelia seemed content to come to France often? Simone was happy with the current arrangement, but she did engage Amelia in her flights of fancy.

Amelia was disappointed, but let it go. "I'll be back soon then," she said to Simone. "I do so adore our time together."

Amelia left the following day, and Simone felt glad her flat was empty except for herself and her books again. She lit a cigarette, opened up some Hegel, and sat in her favorite chair, exhausted but blissful.


## 3.

In January of 1936, Simone received a letter from Amelia asking her once again to visit the States. Amelia had some time off in the Spring and would love to see Simone. She could even invite Sartre if that made her more comfortable.

Simone sat with the letter for a week before responding. She felt it was time for a little truth.

"I'm sorry, Amelia, I simply cannot. Sadly, the timing for a trip across the ocean is horrendous. Jean-Paul has just finished the rough draft of his novel, and we've been going through every sentence with a razor. I hesitate to abandon him when he is so close to accomplishing his opus. My place must be with him right now."

A few weeks later, Simone received a response from the aviator promising to visit in the fall. Amelia's disappointment was evident in every word, but it was a long letter detailing her day to day life. Amelia talked about her house, her stepson, and her airplanes, which she described like jewels. She reiterated her plan to fly around the whole globe and said she hoped the opportunity would present itself soon.

The two of them began a regular correspondence, though Amelia's letters tended to be longer and more frequent. Simone would describe Sartre's progress with the novel, as well as her efforts to write a book of her own. Amelia would respond trying to compare their art to her navigation of the clouds. While Simone enjoyed the distraction of the letters, she found that sometimes the two of them were talking at each other, rather than to each other.

*

Amelia, true to her promise, visited that fall. The trip was enjoyable until an unfortunate disagreement plagued them on Amelia's last night. After they had spent the day in the city, exploring the market and the nearby marina, Simone suggested they have dinner at Sartre's. Amelia was annoyed he was included in their last celebration of the trip.

Amelia spoke little throughout the meal. After dinner, instead of staying to listen to music, Amelia claimed she had a headache and would like to go back to Simone's flat to rest. The goodbye with Sartre was terse. When Simone and Amelia returned to Simone's house, Amelia asked Simone to put on music, so they could dance.

"I thought your head hurt," said Simone, looking for rest herself.

"Sartre makes my head hurt," responded Amelia.

Simone ran her tongue along the top row of her teeth. "He made a nice dinner for us," she told Amelia.

"He is a fine cook – for an ape."

Simone sensed they were bound for an argument, so she tried to change the subject.

"What time do you depart tomorrow?" she asked.

Amelia wouldn't let it go. "I can't believe you stay with him. He stinks, he's arrogant, and he'll never be anything more than he already is."

"Jean-Paul is an incredible writer," argued Simone.

"Not nearly as incredible as you are, yet you spend all your time helping him at a cost to yourself!"

"He is a great philosopher," said Simone. "The world just doesn't know it yet."

"I don't understand you," said Amelia. "You are so brilliant, and you claim to rail against the bourgeoisie, but your relationship with Sartre proves you are nothing more than a hypocrite."

"You're the one who's in a loveless marriage," Simone pointed out.

"Putnam is very good to me," Amelia told her. "And he lets me do what I want. I'm here, aren't I?"

"I do what I want to as well, Amelia," said Simone.

"Then why don't you visit me in the states?"

"Perhaps I don't want to." The truth hung in the air.

The fight left them both feeling raw. Simone felt that a part of Amelia that had been hidden was now revealed.

Later that night, as they lay in bed together, Amelia apologized.

"I will fly around the world next year," Amelia told Simone, "and when I land in Paris, will you be there?"

"I will," said Simone, now feeling affectionate.

They kissed. But Simone couldn't shake the thought that it would be the last time they made love.

*

Their parting was awkward rather than typically bittersweet; after all, they had never argued before. Before her cab arrived, Amelia paced around the flat anxiously. When she heard the car horn, she embraced Simone tightly.

"I know you hate the word, but I do love you, Simone de Beauvoir. And I want, no, I need all of you for the rest of my life." Amelia's voice was shaky.

"I know my dear, I know," said Simone.

"I'll be back soon, I promise." She did not mention Simone visiting the States.

Amelia opened the door to the house, and Simone followed her to the curb. They embraced one final time before Amelia opened the taxi door.

"Goodbye, my dear," said Amelia.

"Goodbye," said Simone, feeling the word was so weak, but having nothing else to say.

The cab sped off.

A week later, Simone received a telegram from Amelia.

"Arrived safely. Miss you more than I can stand. I adore you forever."

Simone did not immediately return a telegram. She waited, and finally composed a letter thanking Amelia for her visit and her devotion. She kept a casual air in the correspondence and spoke of her latest theories. Still, she signed the letter with a kiss.

*

Christmas came. Simone received a portrait of Amelia, strangely in a skirt, accompanied by a letter. Amelia opened it with a declaration of love, followed by talk about her recent goings-on, and promised she was going to come to visit as soon as she could, to resolve their difficulties.

Simone wrote back feigning ignorance and denying any such difficulties.

Amelia replied, complaining of Sartre again, and of Simone's unwillingness to commit more to their relationship.

"I so want a visit from you, darling, it would make everything, just… glow," Amelia wrote.

Simone, feeling a little intruded upon, wrote back with her old trite excuses hoping that Amelia would probe no further.

"I've given you all I can give," she wrote. "And I do want to visit, but I cannot now or anytime soon. Things are simply too busy here."

In her next letter, Amelia rebuked Simone. It was as if they were back in Simone's flat on the evening before Amelia's departure.

"There is more of you to give, you just do not know it," she wrote. "Or if you do know it, you do not allow it. Or, if you do allow yourself, Sartre does not. I do not know. I give you so much and ask for so little! Can you not tell me you <u>adore</u> me as I adore you?"

The letter ends on that note, with "adore" underlined both times. The question lingered in Simone's mind for days. Perhaps she did not adore Amelia. Simone realized the affair had run its course.

Simone replied, "Perhaps we should not correspond anymore. I believe that, despite my hopes, you have fallen jealously in love with me. I told you when we began, I am possessed only by myself. I do carry sentiment for you, but I do not want to hurt your feelings or break your heart. Further correspondence may cause you too much pain, and I cannot be the one responsible for bringing hurt into your life.

Amelia's response arrived rapidly. "Please do not stop writing to me, my darling. I agree I am hopeless with the thought of you, but such a breakage will ruin me. You may trim only so many limbs off a tree. Don't you think if you adore me a little, you could learn to adore me a little more? I sigh now, as I feel this scrawl and ink do not communicate what I wish to. I will come again, soon, to France, and see you, if you want it."

Once again, Amelia underlined both cases of "adore."

It was April 1937, and in the spirit of rebirth, Simone was considering not replying to Amelia's pleas. However, as the truth of the situation dawned on her, she felt sorry for Amelia. Simone may have considered such possessiveness and jealousy a weakness, but she was compelled to empathize with Amelia and her inquisitive, compassionate, and always devoted heart.

Simone took a long time to compose the perfect letter.

"I'm sorry, my dear, dear friend, but I'm afraid I think it best that we do not see each other soon, or correspond as we have until we have let these emotions between us burn themselves out. I have enjoyed my time with you beyond measure, and while I loathe saying goodbye to you, I fear I am only drawing out your pain. Please do not come. Please do not write to me again soon. Yours, Simone."

*

Summer came, and Amelia did not respond. Simone, comforted by her happy memories, considered the matter closed. Sartre had finally completed his novel, *Nausea*, and been offered a teaching post in Paris. Simone would move with him.

Everything was as it should be.

In July, Simone sat in the same café in Paris where she had first met Amelia. She picked up a newspaper with a startling headline — the first female aviator attempting a global flight had disappeared and was presumed dead, along with her navigator. Searchers found no trace of her. She was gone.

Amelia Earhart was dead?

Simone lifted her hand to her heart, gasping. It was impossible to breathe. She stared at the newspaper in disbelief, her fingers trembling as they clenched the paper. She felt lightheaded, and her eyesight darkened as though she might faint. The newspaper fell from her hand as she reached for her tea to take a sip, trying to regain herself.

Sartre came back from the toilet.

"Darling, you are sickly pale, are you alright? You look like you've seen a ghost!" He took her hand in his.

"No," she whispered. "I have only been informed of one."

She showed him the article.

"My goodness!" he exclaimed. "I can't believe it. That's terrible! Surely there must be some trace of her somewhere!"

"There's nothing," Simone says. "It's all gone."

*

All was not gone; Simone had her memories of Amelia, and she would take comfort in them until the day she died. She promised herself she would write a great novel about Amelia. She would write about her passions, her unbelievable determination, and the soft curls of her hair.

It was a week after Simone read the headline, after the grief had taken root in Simone's heart, when Simone received Amelia's final letter, postmarked the day before her fateful flight.

"My dear Simone. If only I could talk to you right now. I feel as though I could make everything work with just my will, but I know that emotion is an illusion. You must never have truly loved me. You are incapable of loving me. You might be incapable of loving anyone.

"But I love you. I love you more than you will ever know. I'm leaving for my flight soon, but I will not return. This is it. I'm going to crash my plane where no one will ever find me, and no one will ever know where I have gone or why. Except you. I'm hoping this burden might trick you into loving me, into feeling something like the way I feel for you. I don't know what else to do. Without you, I am nothing. I don't want to live. I don't even want to fly. Goodbye, Simone. Goodbye."

*

That night, Simone slept at Sartre's house. The emptiness of her flat was too loud. Everywhere she looked, there was a memory of Amelia. Simone snuggled against Sartre's warm body, and, once he was asleep, she cried. She could feel a sharp pain in her chest, and unrest in her belly. Was it guilt? Or had Amelia been successful, and tricked her into love?

She thought of Amelia constantly for a long while.

As the years passed, the grief faded, and she never wavered in her commitment to Sartre. She helped him with his work, helped him with his life, helped him with his sexual affairs. They never married, never had children, and always kept two separate households.

As she grew old, she sometimes thought of Amelia and remembered their time together fondly.

No one knew what had happened to Amelia Earhart. People searched and found nothing. Conspiracies arose and were traded amongst people fascinated with the aviator.

Simone burned the letters.

She is buried in Paris, next to Sartre.

# The Imperial Frost of W. Somerset Maugham

### 1.

It was outdoors at a café in Geneva, Switzerland, in September 1915. The morning breakfast crowd was boisterous as customers conversed, ruffled newspapers, and clinked silverware and plates. Pedestrians streamed by on the street, glancing at the people in the café to see if there was someone they knew, or wanted to know. The air was filled with the buttery scent of freshly bake croissants and the bitter, roasted odor of strong coffee. A great splash of sunlight swooped between the buildings and lit up the small square opposite the café, painting pigeons in chiaroscuro.

"Switzerland is beautiful this time of year," Somerset sighed.

He sat at one of the rickety cast-iron tables with a female companion, Mrs. Baxter, a beautiful, middle-aged blond woman who was a wife to a respected British diplomat. She laughed at his observation. She was one of those beautiful women who was also blessed with a pretty, crystalline laugh, but despite her naturally rosy cheeks and practically invisible laugh lines, she was skinny as a bird's leg, and her wrists had a sort of thin, rectangular, piston-like shape giving her beauty a utilitarian flaw. Mrs. Baxter was dressed finely – though still wearing a straw summer hat in mid-September – and an ornately engraved silver cigarette holder was held daintily between her gloved fingers. She didn't so much blow smoke out as let it spill from her mouth, letting it slowly dissipate around her.

"My dear Mr. Maugham," she said, "Switzerland is *always* beautiful."

Somerset Maugham – summoned to Geneva at the behest of England herself – was a spy, posing as himself, a famous British novelist and playwright. Recruited by his cousin in the British Foreign Service, Somerset was the perfect clandestine operator – a masterful observer, capable of flippancy during the most serious situations, never skittish; and as a famous artist, could believably flutter across the continent, unfettered by bourgeois sensibilities or loyalties, with his true allegiance hidden behind artistic dalliance. He had only performed one mission so far, in Spain, a trifle really, but he had been told that this new mission would be more dangerous. Somerset was filled with excitement.

Mrs. Baxter, cutting the pleasantries short, placed a grainy photo of a hard-looking Indian man on the table in front of Somerset. It impressed him that a woman was his handler, but he supposed women had been involved in espionage since its invention. "This is Virendranath Chattopadhyaya, alias 'Chatto,'" Mrs. Baxter said. "The son of a doctor, educated at Oxford, speaks almost a dozen languages. Somehow, he became a revolutionary.

He is trying to overthrow the British Raj in India by any means necessary. England without India is unthinkable."

Somerset scrutinized the photograph, grazing its edges with the tips of his fingers scientifically – touching a photograph helped him remember it. 'Chatto' was dressed in a coal gray suit, with his hair parted severely over his forehead. He had a small nose, thin lips, and protruding cheekbones, and he grimaced at the photographer and eternity with verve.

"Interesting looking chap," Somerset said, sipping at his coffee.

"Yes, he is very interesting," she agreed. "He is involved in several illegal activities, including the trade of arms along the Indian coast. He has incited riots and is currently seducing Indian students studying at European universities with nationalistic dreams of an independent India. He is creating quite a resistance movement. We believe his allies are trying to convince the Kaiser to help overthrow the Raj, and weaken the British Empire."

"That won't do at all," Somerset said, not sure if any of this interested him yet.

"No, it won't," Mrs. Baxter laughed guardedly. "We have been after Chatto for years. He is very clever. He has slipped through every trap we have laid for him. But we were hoping you might help." Mrs. Baxter reached into her purse and pulled out another photograph and placed it next to Chatto's. "Now… this man might be the answer to our prayers."

Somerset touched this photograph more gently. It was a candid picture of a young Indian man standing in crisp tennis clothes, sporting a confident, devilish smile.

"This is Aarav Pradhan," said Mrs. Baxter. "He is an impressionable young man. He is Chatto's distant cousin, on his mother's side. Chatto depends on him to navigate younger upper class Indian social circles and recruit powerful young students."

"It seems Pradhan is your key to the lock," Somerset pointed out.

"Exactly. And I will tell you why – intelligence reveals that Pradhan is a homosexual." Mrs. Baxter punctuated this last piece of information with a raise of her eyebrow, as if to say, 'like you.'

"I see," said Somerset, drawing on his own cigarette, and blowing smoke into the air. It seemed the British government knew about his inclinations, despite his best efforts. He could easily be thrown into prison for his proclivities, but it seemed the Crown would rather use them to its advantage. He tried to play it calmly. "And what are you suggesting?" he asked her.

"Pradhan seems to prefer older, British men," Mrs. Baxter told him. "I am sure you will have no trouble becoming his friend."

Somerset smiled like he was holding a poor hand of cards. "That makes it all suddenly so clear, darling," he said. "I'm sure we will be great friends."

"Yes," Mrs. Baxter grinned. "Crystal clear. I am glad you see that, Mr. Maugham."

*

Somerset's target had been seen frequenting *En Compagnie des Béliers* since his arrival – a very exclusive night club for men on the rue Voltaire, where patrons had to present either their membership card or a signed invitation to pass through the gilded doorway. If Somerset was going to meet Aarav Pradhan as a matter of happenstance, *En Compagnie des Béliers* was the place to do it. There was no difficulty in procuring a membership for Somerset; in fact, it turned out he already had one.

It was just past nine o'clock when he arrived, stepping down from the fiacre in one of his best suits, his hair combed back with hair wax and his thin mustache perfectly manicured. Somerset was not a naturally attractive man – short, a little rotund, with fat in his jowls that had accompanied him since birth. But – it was the little touches, he believed, that brought out one's inner beauty – the freshly pressed handkerchief, the impeccably shaven neck, and, most importantly, the expensive, sophisticated scent. He had charm.

The first thing he noticed upon entering the club was the vivacious black jazz singer on a raised stage — she couldn't be older than twenty — swaying in a pale yellow dress and singing in fast, raspy tones. The music was intoxicating; although, every time Somerset visited such an establishment, all he could hear in his head were Satie's Gymnopédies. The orchestra was small, but the drummer was overly enthusiastic, like a child stomping through puddles of noise.

Clubs such as these existed since before Mighty Athens, and men congregated here to revel in their shared love of other men. Over the centuries, the accoutrements changed – here the tall windows were covered in thick, purple curtains, so people inside wouldn't be seen by the outside world; large, low-hanging chandeliers shimmered with angelic light; a horseshoe bar dominated half of the space; and a dance floor the other half. Amiable men danced hesitantly together or gathered around the bar like drops of water clinging happily to glass. At *En Compagnie des Béliers,* what hadn't changed over the course of human history was the surprising size of the crowd, the laughter, the gentle touches feigning to be absentminded, and men bending their faces toward other men. Sexual relations between men were the antitheses of mechanism – there was no purpose to any of it other than pleasure. And yet… there was still so much danger — reptiles abounded in places where people were looking for love.

It didn't take long to find Pradhan – he was the only Indian in the club, and he was dressed in a cream suit that exclaimed amongst the ashen garments of the other men. Pradhan stood at one end of the bar surrounded by two lecherous old Germans who were attempting to entice him into God knows what. Somerset took a long look at his target – Pradhan's photograph had not been entirely truthful about how beautiful and young he was – and the deep, dark ochre color of his skin gleamed in the club's diaphanous light. Pradhan's face would no doubt be soft, with the barest invisible fuzz upon it – it was not a face that needed to be shaved more than once a week. Pradhan was not tall, but he was lithe, angular, and as he laughed nervously in front of the Germans, he ran his long fingers through his silky hair.

This would not do. Somerset had a mission; but to see such beauty wasted on decrepit, obviously impotent creatures was against his principles. This would take a complex strategy — he had to maneuver Pradhan away from the Germans while also giving him a dazzling first impression.

He ordered a drink. He paid the bartender to give Pradhan another glass of whatever he was drinking – Irish whiskey with water, the bartender told Somerset. He watched as the bartender gave Pradhan his drink and pointed in Somerset's direction.

Somerset's eyes met Pradhan's. Pradhan smiled, looking at Somerset quizzically, but also in amusement. Somerset gave Pradhan a friendly, confident smirk. One of the Germans said something, extending his salacious talon to lay upon Pradhan's forearm to get his attention. Pradhan broke the stare with Somerset.

Somerset swallowed the last of his drink and ordered another. He made his way through the crowd to where Pradhan was standing with the Germans, as Pradhan took happy but slightly furtive looks in his direction.

"Gentlemen!" Somerset spoke to the Germans as he arrived. "Thank you for entertaining my dear friend while I was detained by a hapless driver."

"Your friend?" one of the Germans asked Pradhan, as the other sized Somerset up.

"Yes, my good friend," said Pradhan, looking into Somerset's eyes.

"And we *must* be going," said Somerset. "We have a dinner to attend in, oh," he looked at his watch. "An hour. We were meeting for an *aperitif.*"

"But we're just getting started," said the second German in a thicker accent than the first.

"Perhaps if my driver had been less of a fool, I would have arrived here at a decent time, and we would have had time to chat," said Somerset. "And, I would not have had to keep my good friend waiting. We are late for a colloquy we both must attend – before our dinner, of course."

Pradhan looked at him in bemused confusion.

"A colloquy?" The first German asked.

"Yes," confirmed Somerset. "And, after all… we *are* at war, you know."

*

"A colloquy?" Pradhan asked over the sound of the band once they were halfway across the club.

"A conversation."

"What conversation?"

Somerset smiled. "The one we are having right now."

Light bloomed across Pradhan's face as his lips spread into an amused smile. "Thank you for the drink," he said. "And for the rescue."

"I admit I did it for selfish purposes. I wanted your attention."

"You have it." Pradhan examined Somerset closely. "You are an Englishman. What are you doing in Geneva?"

"I could ask you the same. Educated at Oxford, I presume?"

"Of course. And you?"

"I was not so fortunate, darling. I studied abroad."

Pradhan bent his neck slightly as he considered what Somerset said. "I suppose I can relate to that," he said. "But you never answered my question."

"Ah," said Somerset. "Actually, you might consider me sort of a professional meanderer."

Pradhan laughed. "And what does that entail?"

"I am a writer."

"Are you? That *is* exciting. What is your name? Have I heard of you?"

"Perhaps. My name is W. Somerset Maugham."

"Indeed! I have heard of you, Mr. Maugham. *Liza of Lambeth* was a dear companion to me on an interminable and miserable trip to Scotland I took two years ago. I dare say I would not have survived my ordeal without it."

Warmth spread across Somerset's chest down into his belly. "You may call me Will. I am honored you have read my trifle of a book."

"It was no trifle, Will!" Pradhan grinned at Somerset greedily. "I am Aarav, Aarav Pradhan." He extended his hand.

They shook. Aarav's skin was smooth and warm. For a brief moment as their hands clasped, they looked into each other's eyes with hungry insistence and fairytale hopes. As they released their grip, Somerset ran a finger down Aarav's wrist.

"It is a great pleasure," Somerset said.

"The pleasure is mine, sir. I have not met one person of substance during my stay in Geneva."

"And what has brought you to Switzerland?"

"I liaise with Indian students at universities across the continent. It is difficult with the war, but there is still work to be done."

"Fascinating. Your social calendar must keep you quite engaged."

"Not as engaged as I would like," Aarav smiled, as the singer finished another song and applause spread across the club. Some men hooted. The singer smiled, clapped her own hands together, and blushed.

"*Merci à vous tous!*" she said to the crowd.

The applause continued as the orchestra left the stage.

"She has a beautiful voice, but I think she needs to work on her French, what do you say?" Somerset chuckled to Aarav.

"French with an American twang," Aarav laughed in response. He smiled at Somerset, hope in his eyes. "Can I buy you a drink?"

"Actually, with the band departed, I have to say my interest has diminished for drinking watered-down liquor in a club whose heyday has long since passed," said Somerset. "Worse, it just so happens that I have a bottle of fine brandy at my hotel that is so luscious you think about it for days afterward."

"Where are you staying?"

"*Hotel d'Angleterre.*"

"That's not far from here," Aarav observed.

"No, it's not," Somerset agreed. "My room has a lovely view of the lake… and the *Jet d'Eau*… If you care to join me, it's just a short ride."

"I would love to," Aarav smiled.

They exited the club and picked from the line of fiacres waiting outside. Aarav climbed up first as Somerset spoke softly to the driver in French. Once they were settled, the driver gently whipped the stirrups, and curved the carriage down the street. The horse's hooves clopped against the stones of the ground as the wooden wheels of the carriage creaked. Somerset pressed his leg against Aarav's, as the carriage rumbled beneath them. Aarav shivered.

"Are you cold?" Somerset asked.

"A little. I've never gotten used to European weather."

"It can be dreadful."

The wheels went over a bump, shaking Somerset and Aarav against each other. Somerset placed his hand on Aarav's thigh. He could feel the heat of Aarav's skin through the thin linen, as well as the muscles trembling beneath his fingers. Aarav leaned into Somerset and breathed into his neck.

"This is dangerous," he sighed.

"Yes, darling," Somerset said, keeping close watch on the driver. "It is."


## 2.

"Did you always want to be a writer?"

"Yes. I mean… I knew, without a doubt, when I was fourteen. But it was impossible. I studied to be a doctor."

"You practiced medicine?"

"For a time."

"What was that like?"

"Very sad, darling."

"You quit."

"I had to quit. The things I saw will haunt me to my grave. I could not bear it anymore. I wrote because I had no choice, because otherwise my talent would dissipate, and the real me would disappear."

"You have been very successful."

"Yes. But I earned it, years of writing at night after long days breathing in the odors of sores and prescribing medicines that wouldn't work. *I* did it, not anyone else."

"And now you are free."

"Free? I suppose I am. I am not as rich as some men, but I am richer than most. I can roam where I want. Start a family and send my children to Oxford."

"Is that something you want?"

"Lord no."

"I would like to have a daughter."

"You would?"

"But I don't think I could ever... love a woman. My parents have already picked out my wife. They picked her a long time ago."

"I have heard that is an Indian custom."

"Yes. And it may be a good match. But... I am who I am."

"So, you will go through with it?"

"I cannot imagine a world where I do not."

"Do you think you will be lonely, darling?"

"I imagine I will be. Are you lonely?"

"I have my own… abstruse… melancholy. But right now? No, I am not lonely."

*

In less than a fortnight, Somerset was in love. It was a torturous blessing. His heart beat faster even when he was not in Aarav's presence. Butterflies took flight in his stomach. He would catch himself sometimes, sitting at his typewriter, or riding the hotel lift, or in the middle of breakfast; and he'd be lost in some preposterous daydream about Aarav – going to an opera in London with him, traveling across the sea to America, waking together on a warm beach. And the desire, the constant desire, burning in every cell in his body from his fingertips to his toes.

Aarav lived in a boarding house for Indian men in Saint-Leger. He was usually occupied in the evenings, but around noon, Somerset would meet him in front of the Cathédrale Saint-Pierre. The gothic, bone-white building was childishly solemn during Somerset's joyful reunions with his lover. When they were feeling restful, they would take lunch at one of the many restaurants in the area, where they would drink wine and tell each other stories. When they were feeling amorous, the two of them would make a quick route to Somerset's hotel. The days passed, and the weather slowly grew colder.

One day, when there was a particularly frigid wind coming off the lake, Somerset entered the ancient church to wait for Aarav. He stood beneath the chapel's towering ceilings, taking in the colorful angels floating in a blue sky brandishing intricately painted trumpets and harps waiting to sound.

"Are you a believer?" Aarav whispered into Somerset's ear, having snuck up behind him.

"You're here!" Somerset showed a luxurious smile. He wanted to throw his arms around Aarav and kiss him on the lips.

They stood in front of each other, holding themselves back.

"So?" Aarav repeated. "Are you a believer?"

Somerset sighed, turning to the altar. "Sometimes, sometimes not," he answered. "I told you my parents died when I was just ten years of age. I was sent to live with my uncle, who was a vicar in Kent, in a little seaside town called Whitstable. He was devout... and cruel, capable of smiling warmly at the village ladies in the garden in one moment, and in the next thrashing me within an inch of my life when no eyes watched. While I believe in the... divine... I hesitate to condone a system that elevates bad people to positions of leadership."

"I understand," Aarav said.

Somerset thought for a moment. "I was in a foreign place – I had spent most of my life in France, and Whitstable was absolutely dreary. The sea was too tempestuous to enjoy, and the people were loathsome – gossiping, condemning, ridiculing, with suspicious eyes and snarling mouths. Absolute loneliness either leads to desperate religiousness or devout despair. I followed the path of despair – I kept my head down, studied, escaped."

Aarav pressed his lips together and smiled reassuringly. "My parents were Hindu," he said. "But they raised me as a Christian, despite not following the faith themselves. They thought it would benefit my future… to be more Western. I cannot say I ever truly believed, but I appreciate the beauty of the religion… the ritual, the tradition. I suppose… my parents did it because they loved me, and wanted the best for me."

"You've been baptized?"

"I have."

"I think," said Somerset, "That all of Christianity boils down to the innate desire that someone, out there, REALLY knows us, all that we are — and forgives us. Can you blame people for wanting that?"

"Do you think God forgives men like you and I?"

Somerset shook his head, incredulous but also a bit bashful. "God created us, did he not? Why would he fashion us in this form only to test us or punish us? Why would he single out our souls for such treatment, and not everyone else's?"

Aarav breathed out after he absorbed what Somerset had said. "In the Hindu scriptures, there are two gods, Ashwini and Kumar. Though identical, they are not brothers, and they are always together. They never part, not even when they sleep. These stories made me feel as though that God had an awareness of boys like me, that I wasn't an anomaly or a demon's handiwork."

A blast of cold wind streamed through the church. Someone must have opened the front doors. A strange combination of grief and reverence filled Somerset's heart.

"This place is very old," he said.

"Everything is old in Europe," Aarav smiled back.

Somerset laughed. "Only to the young."

Despite Aarav's maturity, he still betrayed the vacuity and alacrity of his age. But it was moments like these, when the boy was profound but also innocent in his immortal illusions, that Somerset loved him most. He had known other young men like Aarav – but they had not *been* Aarav, and to be alike is not to be the same. The weight of Somerset's feelings for this young man towered over the many infatuations he had indulged in over the course of his life; sometimes he would wake in the late night, and slip out of bed while Aarav was still sleeping, and he would sit half-naked in the arm chair, holding his hands out in front of him to examine them, astonished at what they possessed.

"Hungry?" Aarav asked, dispelling Somerset's revelry.

"Yes!" Somerset replied. "I know a restaurant near here that has a veal and mushrooms that is so delectable, you think you are dining on ambrosia on Mount Olympus."

*

"So, what do you have on Pradhan?" Mrs. Baxter asked Somerset.

The rain poured down as they drank their coffee inside the café. A late lunch crowd dined on crêpes and the café's famous autumn salad. Despite the miserable weather outside, the patrons were obviously elated to be dry and dining, the harmony of their voices like a lilting waltz.

"Oh," said Somerset. "He is just a lad. Harmless."

"These people are not harmless, Mr. Maugham."

"I think you have Aarav mistaken for someone else."

"I assure you, *Pradhan* is exactly whom we say he is."

"He is not dangerous!"

Mrs. Baxter raised an eyebrow. "I believe you have become quite enamored with Pradhan, Mr. Maugham. Perhaps you are not seeing clearly in this matter."

"I am not *enamored* with him," Somerset argued, though he knew he was. "I have done what you asked and become his friend. I am simply telling you – he is a good person, incapable of what you are accusing him of doing."

"Has he mentioned Chatto?"

"He has not."

Mrs. Baxter grimaced. "Chatto is a murderer and a threat to the British Empire."

"And I am telling you, Aarav Pradhan has nothing to do with him."

Mrs. Baxter took a long drag from her cigarette. "I am beginning to have my doubts about you, Mr. Maugham. Do you realize what is at stake here?"

Somerset's heart sank. He realized Mrs. Baxter's interests were not his interests.

"Aarav Pradhan is abetting a known insurrectionist," Mrs. Baxter continued. "He is a threat to England. You have to think of England as a stern father – India is like a child, and like a child, it must be guided and protected. I think you had better come to your senses… and quickly. You need to do what you promised your country you would do."

"I never promised anything," Somerset growled in a whisper. He wasn't going to genuflect in front of her.

"Neither did we, Mr. Maugham. Neither did we."

Somerset sipped his coffee, shocked to find something he loved suddenly tasted so bitter.

"I will do what I can," he said.

*

Aarav invited Somerset to a dinner party hosted by a professor at the University of Geneva who specialized in oriental studies. Aarav said he wanted Somerset to meet his friends. Due to Aarav's schedule that day, they agreed to meet at the dinner party, a decision Somerset would later regret.

The address for the party was in Les Tranchées. Feeling adventurous, Somerset tried Geneva's steam tramway, which was a delight – he couldn't believe such beastly transport could operate so quietly, and the combination of silence and motion made him think of Jules Verne. But he got off at the wrong stop, finding himself in an unfamiliar area of the city, getting lost among streets he had never seen before. He looked at his watch; he had plenty of time. He hired a fiacre, but then the coachman got lost around the university. He was late to meet Aarav, and the lie he had told the lecherous Germans about an incompetent coachman had belatedly come true. Finally, thinking he knew better, he paid the coachman and stepped down to the street; it was getting dark now, but Somerset had a good feeling about the map in his mind of the surrounding area. He found his destination, but it took more time.

It was a modest, three story house that in the dimming light looked not entirely dissimilar to his expectations of it. The street was silent, but he could hear voices coming from the front room of the house. He wished he had come with Aarav. He rang the doorbell, and the voices quieted. A young Indian man in a blue suit answered the door, looking surprised anyone would ring the doorbell at this point of the evening.

"Good evening," said Somerset, "I apologize, but I was invited to dinner and I am terribly, terribly late. I am a friend of Mr. Aarav Pradhan."

The young man lifted his chin up in acknowledgement. He told Somerset to come in, come in; but he did not know where Aarav was.

About a dozen Indian men were spread across the room's furniture, lounging around after their dinner in gastronomic, soporific bliss, gingerly holding drinks and cigarettes, a cavalcade of brown faces. Was he the only white man in this house? It was a startling feeling. Despite what the gentleman at the door said, Somerset scanned all their faces; they looked at him with bemusement and suspicion.

He stepped lightly through the room as the murmur of conversation returned delicately. Piano notes spilled down the stairs at the back of the room – someone was playing the main theme from Mahler's 3$^{rd}$ on a piano on the second floor. It was not the most dexterous performance; and the haphazardly ominous melody precariously floated in the air like a monster wobbling on a bicycle.

Past the staircase, through the amber light of a hallway, he found a large study to his left and a closed door to his right from which issued the sound of pot scrubbing – that must have been the kitchen. To the back was a bathroom and a door that led to the back garden. Through the window, he saw the polite flare of orange cigarette light, and low voices came from that direction. He pulled open the door and found three men standing together with drinks – two Indians and a white man. He quickly recognized one of the Indians was Aarav, and a big smile came to his lips. He also realized the other Indian man was from the other photograph Mrs. Baxter had showed him – Chatto.

"Aarav!" Somerset's voice always betrayed his love when he said Aarav's name. At least, that's what it sounded like to him – especially right now. As he looked into the adoring crowd of Aarav's eyes, he didn't care.

"William! I am so glad you came!"

"I apologize for my tardiness," said Somerset. "I got lost. Multiple times. I was afraid Virgil was going to appear to guide me out of the dark wood of Geneva and escort me to Hell!" He smiled at his own cleverness, but despite Aarav's short chuckle, the other two men – though probably knowing his reference to Dante's *Inferno* – were not impressed, and he told himself not to be so loquacious.

"William," Aarav said, "these are two of my friends. This is the esteemed Professor Léonce Reverdin, of the University of Geneva. And this is my dear cousin, mentor, and friend, Virendranath Chattopadhyaya – but everyone calls him Chatto. This," he gestured to the professor and Chatto, "is William Somerset Maugham, the writer."

Chatto was shorter than Somerset had imagined, squat; but his torso was wide, and his rumpled suit's sleeves were too short for his arms. He had keen, cold eyes, and small, nervous hands. Professor Reverdin however was tall, lanky, in an oversized suit; he wore a comically large mustache that looked like it was going to leap from his face and scurry under a piece of furniture.

"I am delighted to meet you both," said Somerset.

"Charmed," said Chatto, his voice dripping with condescension. The Swiss professor only smiled.

"I suppose I missed dinner," Somerset, banally stating the obvious, but only because he felt his stomach gently grumbling.

"Maybe we could have the cook fix you something," Aarav suggested, sounding concerned. He looked at Prof. Reverdin, who shrugged.

"No, that is perfectly alright," said Somerset. He smiled amiably, stealing a glance at Chatto – he realized the man was displaying the same grimace he had in his photo.

"We were just discussing India," said Chatto. "Surely, Mr. Maugham, you have an opinion on it?"

As a British man of a certain age and income, Somerset of course had his opinions about India. But compared to his contemporaries he was quite liberal. In this situation, however, he realized he was in strange territory and decided to be glib. "I'm a writer," chuckled Somerset. "My opinions are like the Greek gods — passionate, spiteful — and fickle."

"And of course the inhabitants of Olympus were not known for their compassion," Chatto snidely observed.

"I would argue, sir, that compassion and empathy are the main concerns of my art." Somerset was in no mood for histrionics.

"Books are cheaply sacred," Chatto muttered.

Somerset felt the heat rising up the back of his neck. "If a work of literature has a modicum of greatness, it cannot be disregarded." He seethed.

"Gentlemen," said Aarav, hesitantly, "Surely we can agree culture is integral to civilization."

"You know," said Chatto, "When a *hostile* power colonizes a defenseless society, it's the culture of the colonized that it destroys first. Libraries are burned, religions are supplanted, and literature is obliterated."

"The English did no such things," said Somerset.

Chatto laughed. "That's the thing about imperial powers – they ply their fairytales not only to their slaves, but also to their citizens."

Somerset eyed the professor, hoping he would come to his aid. Then he looked nervously at Aarav, whose face was frozen in a helpless expression. He had never been so accosted by such a radical.

"I think," said Somerset, "I would be very appreciative if the lady of the house heated some dinner for me after all."

"Of course!" Aarav blurted. "Professor Reverdin, could that be arranged?"

The professor raised his eyebrows, astonished by this development, and obviously disappointed and annoyed.
"Of course," he said. "I will see to it at once."

"If you follow me," Aarav said to Somerset. "You can wash up and I'll introduce you to Madame Reverdin. She's a painter!"

Somerset smiled, and his stomach tingled in anticipation of food, mixed with the tension of his discussion with Chatto. He followed his lover – whom he had never been so thankful for but also so confused about.

*

"You frighten me sometimes."

"*I* frighten you, darling?"

"Yes."

"But why?"

"I do not know. But I feel it."

"I'm harmless!"

"I know. There is just something that…persists."

"I would never hurt you, Aarav."

"I know. I am just telling you what I feel."

"Your friends did not like me."

"I apologize for their behavior. Chatto is very passionate."

"That is madness, not passion."

"Surely you have pity for India?"

"Yes. Of course. But it is improving."

"My people just want to be free."

"But they are free."

"Not free to govern themselves."

"But British rule has elevated the Indian people. British law has brought justice to their society. English education has brought the Indian people into the modern world."

"It is foolish to think India did not have laws before Britain came. It is also false that India was not part of the world before British Imperialism."

"That is not what I said, darling. I am just extolling the benefits of British rule. You must admit it has its advantages."

"Evil can never be justified by its accomplishments. I will tell you this, William. The British have ruled India for so long, the Indian people can no longer imagine their lives without it."

"Can you?"

"I can. Deep in their hearts, my people want to be free. Free to decide their own lives and govern themselves, without merely being numbers on a British ledger."

"I can understand that. I am just saying, it is a very complex situation."

"We have tried petitioning the government for more independence, but England could not care less – not as long as India is profitable. I do not mean to offend, but it is demeaning to be colonized."

"I am not offended. I understand what you are saying."

"Let me tell you something. When I was a boy, no more than ten, all of Calcutta was talking about a planned demonstration against British rule. I didn't understand what was going on, but I knew it was important. My parents forbade me to leave the house, but they could not deter me. After lunch, I claimed I was not feeling well and retired to my room. I snuck out of the window and over the wall of the garden. I ran happily through the city. Thousands of people had gathered in the streets. It was exciting, to be part of something important. Soldiers and police arrived out of nowhere, as though they were lying in wait the whole time. They beat at the crowd with sticks, and I realized I was part of that crowd, that the policemen were dangerous. I couldn't understand why Indian soldiers and policemen would attack their own people when they protested for freedom. Gunshots rang out. A soldier stabbed a man with a bayonet. I still see the arc of that man's body as he fell – you would think he would have just collapsed, but instead he swayed, swinging his arms as his knees bent in a sort of dance. Then he was on the ground, bleeding among the stones and dust. I ran. One of my uncles saw me and rushed me back to my parents' house, scolding me the entire way. Once we arrived home and my uncle had told my parents what happened, they became infuriated, my mother screamed at me – 'There is more than one India, you little fool! You could have been killed!' I felt such shame. But I realized later, it was a good shame, that after a while I was less ashamed of dishonoring my family and more ashamed of my privilege. My blindness."

"That's awful, darling."

"I did not mean to upset you, William."

"I am not upset. There's just so much I do not understand."

"I apologize for becoming so incensed. I do not want to ruin our happiness."


<u>**3.**</u>

What was a face? A window, yes, into infinities. The forehead – capable of surprising expression. The eyebrows, articulate, sharply drawn out of brisk hairs, a marvel of evolution. The twitching skin around the eyes, and the brown eyes themselves, like the richest chocolate. The nose, made of mathematic curves, the center of the face, a peak settled between the full, square cheeks which reach down to the strong jaw. And the lips. Oh god, his lips.

Somerset loved kissing Aarav. His lover's lips were full, sensitive to the smallest, most subtle touch, from the vermillion borders to the wet space between the *Labium superius oris* and *Labium inferius oris*. Aarav never touched cigarettes, so his mouth tasted like the expensive Italian mints he was fond of sucking on, and Somerset reveled in this ambrosial flavor that he knew would haunt him until his death. There's less skin on the lips than the rest of the body, less interference between nerve and touch, and that's why the lips are richer in color – the increased sensitivity makes the blood vessels apparent. The lightheadedness, the tingle in his own lips, all these things combined into a euphoric experience that was beyond affection, beyond desire, something instead that transcended the fallen world and reverberated in the heavens. But those lips – capable of communicating such beauty and sorrow and comedy; and yet – what is hidden in the silences of those same lips, what do they refuse to say?

From there, Somerset would kiss down the chin to the neck, where life pulsed, and Aarav would sigh when Somerset's lips pressed against the soft, gently concave spots adjacent to the Adam's Apple. He would trace a path from the base of the neck to each shoulder, made strong from crew at Oxford, before returning to the center of the chest. Aarav's nipples were dark, rimmed with black hairs that rose and drooped like heavy flowers upon their stems. Somerset's lover's stomach was flat, but soft, and sometimes he would lay his head upon his, resting his hand on Aarav's cool flank as he listened to his lover's inner mechanisms.

Then there was the arc of the pubis, covered with thick hair and descending to the weight and heat of Aarav's sex. The thighs – where the skin was paler than the rest of Aarav's body, and the muscles – crew at Oxford again, what a wonderful sport! – which trembled beneath Somerset's fingers and his kisses. Aarav's knees, bony, and amazingly sort of silly and pathetic in an otherwise Apollonian body. And Aarav's feet, wide, with pointed big toes, and the soft bottoms of his feet, colored like pink sawdust.

*His* Aarav, complete, and in his lover's embrace, Somerset found an ecstasy he had never known before. He didn't know what it was – he had known the comforts of many men, but the light in Aarav's eyes was different; Aarav wasn't the kind of man who looked at the future with a grimace, trading pleasure for obligation. Instead, he took his responsibilities in stride, without resentment; but at the same time, Aarav was a man of hope – he believed in the potential of the future to surprise. All of Somerset's lovers, despite their gifts, despite their wondrous humanity, had an emptiness in their hearts, of one sort of another. But not Aarav. His heart was full. And it was for this reason that Somerset loved him so.

But there was strife.

Things hadn't been the same since the night of the dinner party. An invisible wall had seeped into the spaces between Somerset and Aarav, and new silences descended upon the broaching of certain subjects, insidious in its potential to come up in any conversation, despite Somerset's best efforts, and, it appeared, Aarav's efforts as well. They didn't discuss it. Somerset did not want to upset his lover or the joy they had found together, and even though the two of them had not argued between themselves about India, they had both stepped into spaces that proved precarious. It was all very English, of course, their manners, and while Somerset imagined he and Aarav finding some sort of reconciliation on the delicate subject, he also felt the situation intractable, and as much as his heart wanted to submit to Aarav, there was a separate, hard pulse in his chest, that in his wiser moments he realized was an impervious knot of pride. The two of them had their private world, but outside of that was a larger, stronger world, and in his love for Aarav, Somerset ebbed between boundless sentiment and an unbearable distance that could not be encroached.

*

They were coming out of the cinema on the Rue Azalée after having seen the American director Cecile B. DeMille's moving picture of Bizet's *Carmen*. The theatre had only been half-crowded, but by the oohs and ahs, it had been apparent it was the first moving picture experience for some in the audience.

They stepped out of the theatre onto the sidewalk under the marquee as the other audience members flowed out around them. They had gone into the theatre when it had been still day, and now it was dark. The colors of the real world were astonishing after staring at the black and white film for an hour, and Somerset's eyes felt as though they were having some sort of incommunicable epiphany. He sensed Aarav walking slowly by his side, but they hadn't said anything to each other yet, in a daze, not quite having both feet back in reality after the fantasy of the film.

An automobile streamed past on the street, and Somerset's eyes traced its departure as though it had been an out of place wild animal. "Did you like the film?" he asked Aarav tentatively.

Aarav nodded, but did not speak and did not smile.

Satisfied his lover had enjoyed the film as much as he had, Somerset opened up. "I thought it was quite something. But it was *not* the opera. I will say the production was a banquet for the eyes… of course, Gustave Flaubert invented the cinema…"

Aarav was silent. Perhaps he didn't enjoy the film after all. Somerset took a deep breath. The busy movement of the street in the real world was a little disorienting after the movie, though he could feel himself reacclimatizing himself to reality.

"Would you like an *aperitif* before dinner?" Somerset asked.

"Yes," said Aarav, his eyes absently tracking something down the street. "I would like that."

They found a bistro and decided to take dinner there as well. The *maître de* placed them in a back corner away from a large, boisterous party at a table that took up half the restaurant. Still, the din of loud toasts and laughter carried over, and Somerset and Aarav eyed each other awkwardly as they waited for their drinks. The waiter returned and placed down Somerset's sherry and Aarav's white wine, then mindlessly recited the night's specials. They asked for oysters and time to think about their entrees. The waiter nodded, placed his pad into his apron, and returned to the demanding party at the center of the restaurant.

Aarav was quiet. Somerset tried making small talk – the weather was getting colder, wasn't it, he even saw a woman in a fur coat in the morning today, the nights were almost freezing. Aarav nodded and stared into the distance.

"What is wrong, darling?" Somerset asked.

Aarav rubbed his face with his hands and shook his head. "I suppose I am just tired."

"You have barely spoken a word all night."

"I know. I apologize for not being very much fun."

"Do you want to tell me what is bothering you so?"

Aarav sighed. "I suppose… I am wavering in my commitment to my work."

"How so?"

"I am finding it… less idealistic than I expected."

"But…" Somerset said, tightening his fingers around his wine glass, "Is that not life?"

"I am not saying I am disillusioned. I started doing this because of disillusionment. I am just thinking to myself… is it really worth it?"

"How so?"

"What I give to this… is it worth it? Why am I really doing it? It all feels… futile."

"You have never explained exactly what you do, darling."

"I know. I suppose sometimes it all feels clear, and I know why I am working so hard. But other times, the details become blinding, like I am lost in tall grass without a compass, and my purpose becomes murky."

"You are working towards an independent India."

"Is that an accusation?"

"Not at all. An observation."

"I know it is a difficult subject between us."

"It is nothing compared to my feelings for you," Somerset whispered.

"I remember in the beginning, I was flush with the dream," said Aarav. "But sometimes it appears insurmountable, and I am afraid some of my… associates have been taking more desperate maneuvers toward our goal."

"Meaning?"

"I may be asked to sully my hands."

Somerset took a deep breath. They were silent for a moment and the waiter brought the drinks and oysters.

"Wonderful, darling," Somerset said. He took a sip of his sherry as the waiter gently but quickly laid down the platter of oysters, and then asked Somerset and Aarav what they would like for dinner. Somerset ordered the chicken confit but asked for the roasted potatoes to be darkened until they were crisp. Aarav, his thoughts elsewhere, took a moment and then asked for the lamb shank navarin.

After the waiter departed, Somerset smiled at Aarav, ignoring the urge to take his lover's hand. "Surely you would not be asked to do anything illegal."

Aarav averted Somerset's eyes. "I have to admit I have continued on in my position even though I am aware of the illicit activities of my associates."

"Why?"

"I am not sure you would understand."

"I can try, darling."

Aarav tilted his head towards his right shoulder, in a sort of half shrug, pondering. "You know I love India."

"I know."

"I am just trying to do the right thing."

"We all think we can change the world when we are young."

"Do not condescend to me, Will."

Somerset shook his head apologetically. "I do not mean to. I am just trying to tell you not to take risks you might regret."

He took a sip of his sherry and tried to smile at Aarav, who reached self-consciously to place some oysters on his plate. They were silent for a minute.

"I did some writing today," Somerset spoke, trying to be light.

"Oh?"

"I was very productive."

"What is your story about?"

Somerset reached for some oysters, not having expected Aarav to ask that. His story was about Aarav – but of course in an oblique way. Honestly, Somerset had been in the throes of inspiration for the past few days; this was no ordinary story, but the tale of two men from different cultures whose passion signifies the possibility of reconciliation between all mankind. It was hopeful, poetic, a hidden breath of the lost age of Romanticism, tying the treasured love stories of the past to the smoky, iron present.

"It's nothing," said Somerset. "Just…a trifle."

*

Later that night, they made love. Somerset's room was dark, but the curtains were open; the full moon hung bright in the twinkling black sky, and the virginal light of Artemis shined over them, giving their bodies the eternal shadows of marble statues. But despite Somerset's physical arousal, his mind was elsewhere; it was like his eyes were moving over the stanzas of a poem, but their essence was lost to him. In the end though, he found himself weeping into Aarav's hot, wet shoulder. "I love you so much!" he whimpered breathlessly. "So much!"

Aarav was the type of man who couldn't sleep if someone was touching him, so afterwards their bodies slipped apart and Aarav turned his head to the wall. Somerset listened to Aarav's slowing breath as he tried to think of something to say. His body shivered as his sweat cooled and dried. He noticed the pace of Aarav's breath become rhythmic, and then slowed further until Somerset knew Aarav was asleep. His eyes rested on Aarav's muscled shoulders, pulsing ever so slightly with his breath. Somerset reached across the bed, and after hesitating a moment, traced a finger down Aarav's spine. Aarav did not stir.

It all reminded him of when he himself was in his twenties, and with one of his first male lovers, the much older and immortally rich Lord Marcus Baccus. One night, Somerset awoke in Lord Marcus's ancient, massive bed – a behemoth of comfort with bedposts that reached into the foundations of the earth, and a heap of goose feather pillows that would tumble off the bed as they made love. Somerset found himself completely stretched out like Da Vinci's Vitruvian Man, and turned his head to see Lord Marcus on his side, his head raised on his elbow as he watched Somerset intently.

"What are you doing?" Somerset had asked, a little violated but also flattered.

Lord Marcus smiled silently for a moment. Somerset's sleepy eyes took in his lover – the ruffled hair, the pale, soft shoulders, the coppery freckles visible beneath his thick gray chest hair. Lord Marcus had a sheet wrapped around his waist, while Somerset was naked as an infant. It was summer and the sheet beneath Somerset's back was slightly damp with sweat.

"I am just watching the world tick," said Lord Marcus. "I am… watching you as your heart slowly, but insistently, beats."

"My heart?" Somerset smiled.

"There is no creation more majestic than the human heart," Lord Marcus mused. "Scientists and philosophers praise the brain — thought. The mind." Lord Marcus traced his finger down Somerset's chest. "But it is the emotions that are truly sublime – invisible…intangible… inexpressible…fleeting… consuming… incorruptible. Pure. That is how you know a man, Will. What he loves, what he hates. What he desires. Reason? Imagination? These are simple evolutionary developments. But passion – anger, sorrow, jealousy – these are things Gods feel."

"And what about love?"

"Love!" Lord Marcus raised the back of his hand to his forehead and pretended to swoon. "The greatest phantom of all."

"But surely you have loved?" Somerset protested.

"I have loved… in the past," said Lord Marcus. "Yes, the emotions are pure. They drive our actions. They are omnipotent and ever present. But love is inside you. It does not affect the world. It does not influence fate. And there are many kinds of love – between lovers, between a son and his mother, between a child and his dog. It is the most powerful emotion, and the least controllable; it is like a wild animal, trapped in the civilization of our inhibitions and social mores. And yet, in time, it fades.

And afterwards we tell ourselves, no, that wasn't real love, it was only an illusion, but real love, oh, one day it will come…"

"So…" said Somerset, "Do you not love at all then, now?"

Lord Marcus reached out and cupped Somerset's chin, chuckling sadly. "Narcissists are made, not born, my darling."

Somerset sunk out of his revelry back into bed with Aarav. He stared at his lover and willed him to awake. Aarav did not stir.

## <u>4.</u>

And then it was December. Rain settled over the city, darkening the sky, and sending the citizens of Geneva ducking through the streets with their umbrellas pulled tight over their heads. A bitterly cold wind blew vengefully off the lake; deep puddles of water littered the city's streets, and fiacre wheels would crash through them in noisy splashes while the horses grunted; the sun started setting in the early afternoon, and at night the city was eerily empty as the rain hammered down. Mornings slowly seeped out of the endless nights painfully slow – the top edge of the eastern sky would gradually lighten from black night until the sky was the color of a wet newspaper; and that was as bright as it would get for the rest of the day.

For the first two days, Somerset and Aarav luxuriated in the solitude, staying in Somerset's room only to leave for meals, and sleeping for long hours after bouts of lovemaking. All of their troubles faded away – they were one. Despite the daylong twilight, they kept the lamps off, and milky light gently poured itself in through the windows; the staccato of the downpour was romantic – and it was like time itself had been washed away.

But on the third day, even they were fatigued by the rain. After breakfast they made love, and while their passion had not diminished, a few minutes after they had finished, Aarav sighed loudly and complained about the rain. They slept. In the early afternoon, pinpricks of blue sky appeared in the cloud cover, and shining sabres of light shined down on Geneva. Aarav lifted himself from the bed and took Somerset's hand. The rain was over.

They dressed and left the hotel. It was two o'clock. While it was chilly outside, the sky was a cerulean blue, with blotches of slate-colored clouds slowly pushing to the east. The sun was in its full glory now, and the color yellow, which had been absent for three days, spilled across the city like an overflowing stream. People appeared quickly on the streets, some tentatively holding umbrellas loosely at their sides, and some so exuberant, they had left their coats inside.

Somerset and Aarav decided to take a walk down to the Jet D'eau where Lake Geneva met the River Rhone. The monumental fountain, Geneva's most famous landmark, had originally been created further downstream in 1886, and it had been purely functional, relieving pressure on the hydraulic power plant. It had been moved here in 1891, when its function became less important, and its beauty became supreme. The Jet D'eau shot its white, foamy spray ninety meters into the air, where it seemed to float for the most transient instant, until falling in a haze back to the lake. Somerset and Aarav stood on the Promenade du Lac Léman, and as happy crowds flowed around them, they were silent – Somerset was tired; the rainy days had exhausted him, and he knew they had done the same to his lover. What he wanted to do was reach out and take Aarav's hand, and squeeze Aarav's warm flesh into his own. But such a thing was never to be.

"Look," said Aarav, pointing at the fountain. "A rainbow!"

Underneath the spray of the fountain, where the haze took the shape of a phantom, a wide arch of color floated, an architecture of unbelievable magnificence visible, but intangible. Now, Somerset did reach out for a moment and take Aarav's hand. Aarav's skin was warm, and so soft, pulsing with his life. Their eyes met, and for the briefest second, Somerset felt an otherwise impossible happiness. But he quickly withdrew his hand, looking around to see if anyone had observed them.

"I have to deliver something to Chatto tomorrow," Aarav said.

"What is it?"

"I would rather not say. I could implicate you."

"Implicate me? In what?"

Aarav looked away, fixing his eyes on the Jet D'Eau. "Forgive me my secrecy. I am thinking only of you."

Somerset turned back to the crowd. He caught sight of a young boy in a green suit, running, stumble and fall to his hands and knees. The boy froze for a second as he absorbed what had happened, and then raised himself halfway, examining his hands to see if he was injured.

"This… item you have to deliver. Do you have it now?"

"No. I am going to pick it up tomorrow morning."

Somerset sucked in a deep, slow breath. "You do not have to do it."

Aarav shook his head. "I have considered the same thing. I do have to do it, Will."

"Do not let Chatto corrupt you, darling."

"Chatto is a means to an end," Aarav replied. "Do you not understand? My goal is insurmountable."

"Then that is all the more reason not to endanger yourself."

Aarav took an angry breath through his flaring nose. "You do not understand me."

"Maybe I do not. But I do love you. Very much."

"How can you love someone you do not understand?"

A cold tingle went down Somerset's spine. "We never understand anyone completely. That is a youthful dream."

"Like my dream of a free India?"

"We cannot divert all the waters of the world by ourselves."

"History awaits those who wish to free the unfree," Aarav argued.

"No," said Somerset. "History cannot be trusted."

Aarav scratched his cheek nervously. "You think I am a young fool."

"That is why I love you," Somerset told him. "I myself am a ruined, empty old man. You give me hope, Aarav. But when you are my age you start to look at your life as a series of disappointments and agonies, and you struggle your best to avoid more."

"I have to do something," Aarav said quietly, looking in Somerset's eyes.

"Why?

"Have you never felt like I do?"

"I am not as virtuous as you are."

"You say I am virtuous yet you condescend to me."

"I do not mean to."

"Maybe history cannot be trusted. But we are history – it forms most of what we are, our perspectives, our fears, our social mores. The animal is in there somewhere, but it is a blur, trapped."

"If that is so," said Somerset. "Where does history end and we begin?"

"I do not know."

They were silent.

"Run away with me," Somerset whispered. "We could go anywhere. Across the world. I have plenty of money. We can run away from all this."

"And then would I be your possession?" Aarav asked.

"No! You would just be yourself. Without … all this."

"Will." Aarav placed his hand on Somerset's shoulder. "I am… *all this*."

*

Early the next morning, Aarav awoke and left the bed without a word, dressing methodically as Somerset watched silently. From the dim, leaden blue light coming in through the windows,

Somerset could tell it was going to be an unsympathetically cold day. He peered at the clock on the wall across the room, but it was as if time meant nothing anymore; Aarav was slipping out of his hands, an impermeable heartbreak had filled every atom of the world, in a grim orgy of shattering hopes and lonely despair.

"I'll miss you today," said Somerset, breaking the silence with a platitude that he had uttered other days without a thought other than the elation the eventual reunion would bring. But that had been in an irrevocable past, infused with optimism and an ecstatic longing that seemed as remote as the moon on a moonless night, a golden age so lost to the ages, that the Trojan War seemed like a current event in comparison.

"I'll miss you too," said Aarav, not smiling or turning. Somerset could feel the invincible stone of Aarav's surreptitious plans, hidden deep within his lover, no doubt intertwined with fear, anxiety, and maybe, some excitement. Aarav bent to pick up his socks and then sat upon the edge of the bed.

"Are you nervous, darling?"

Aarav took a second to respond. "Not at all," he said. Somerset knew he was lying. "It's just a trifle," said Aarav, pulling on his socks. "It will be over in a few hours."

"And when will I see you?"

Aarav scratched his cheek. "Tonight, I think?"

"When?" Somerset could hear the trepidation in his voice.

"I do not know what the day will bring."

"But we will see each other?"

"I just cannot think that far ahead, William."

"You said we would see each other tonight."

"I just do not know when."

"I have to have something to hold on to, darling."

Aarav sighed. "Alright. I understand. Let's meet at the cathedral. At eight."

Somerset crawled across the bed to embrace Aarav's shoulders. "Thank you, darling." He kissed Aarav's cheek. Aarav tilted his neck so their foreheads rested against each other.

"I do love you, William."

"Don't say it like we'll never see each other again."

"I'm not. I just want you to know that you are still foremost in my thoughts."

Was this true? Somerset had known this feeling before, at a point in an affair where you're still madly in love, but the realization that it will never work is starting to eat into you like a ravenous rat.

Aarav stood up, pulling himself from Somerset's arms, and turned his head around the room, looking for his shoes. They were under the table. He picked them up, loosened the laces, and stepped into them. "I have to go."

Pain cascaded down from Somerset's heart to his stomach. "I love you!" He exclaimed.

Aarav smiled at last, bending to kiss Somerset. Their lips had known many kisses together, and they could communicate their feelings better with the subtle sensations of their lips than with words. And this kiss was no different – Somerset's lips tugged on Aarav's, fiercely grasping his fleeing lover in a way his arms never could. Somerset felt dizzy; he sucked air through his nose as he gripped Aarav's waist tightly, trying his best not to fall back into the real world that had enveloped him before he had met Aarav.

Finally Aarav broke the kiss, and the Somerset felt everything drop underneath him. Aarav cupped Somerset's cheek with his hand and then looked into his eyes. "I will see you tonight. Eight o'clock. I promise."

Aarav turned to leave.

"Don't go!"

Aarav froze in his steps. "I'm sorry, Will."

He pulled the door open with a creak.

"I'll see you tonight."

*

After Aarav left, Somerset lay motionless in the bed for a few minutes. Would he ever see Aarav again? What had he done wrong? There was a gaping maw in his heart, feasting on his anguish; he had never felt so powerless and lost, it was all gone, he had lost Aarav, it was over. What if he leapt out of bed, ran half-naked down the hotel corridor, rode the painfully slow lift down to the lobby, chased Aarav into the streets, embraced him, never let him go?

Somerset pulled himself out of bed and stood unsteadily. He took slow, short steps to the bathroom, as though the floor might fall out beneath him. He was unprepared for the mirror once he had switched the light on; his desperate visage greeted him like a bloodthirsty Mongol. He sighed and his eyes widened as he looked upon himself – his hair was ruffled, a brown-gray skein of stubble covered his cheeks and chin, and his skin was blotchy. He saw that there was a lilac-colored, coin-shaped bruise in the left hollow of his neck – Aarav. He raised his finger and touched it lightly; it did not hurt. He realized he didn't even have a photograph of Aarav, that he had no keepsakes, they had never bought each other gifts. If he never saw Aarav again, this bruise would be all he had left of him, and it a few days it would fade, disappear, and there would be nothing.

He performed his ablutions, took a bath, and shaved. Afterwards he thought about having breakfast, but he had no appetite – his stomach felt like a falling stone. He sat at his desk and indulged in a glass of brandy; on his empty stomach, the liquor oozed through his belly and its warmth spread into his chest and arms. Before him was his latest manuscript, and his looping script seemed suddenly alien to him, ephemeral and needless.

Nevertheless, he decided he would distract himself with his work. He took up his pen but it felt as though he was holding a piece of trash. His pen point hovered over the paper, overcome with bashfulness and self-disgust. He realized that not even the melodic silence of literature could save him today.

It was turning into a beautiful, cloudless day. This had to be an omen – Aarav would return to him. But time had never moved so slowly.

He stood and gazed at Lake Geneva. The morning sun crashed into the blue waters in an explosion of shimmering rays of light, and Geneva stood majestic around it; antiquity suddenly felt as though it wasn't so far away after all, and Somerset was consumed by the weight of millennia; all the heartbreaks of history descended upon him, like a crowd of vengeful demons, and his knees buckled. He fell to the floor and wept.

*

At ten to seven that night, Somerset could wait no longer, and he descended to the street to hire a fiacre. It was pleasantly warm, or warm compared to the previous days, and the city buzzed with life – people were shopping, gallivanting, off to dine, or just enjoying the air. True winter was no doubt camped with its armies around the city, and the forthcoming siege had people trying to enjoy the last remnants of the autumn.

Somerset's heart pounded with excitement and fear. He had not eaten all day, and his stomach tore loudly at itself and his head was dizzy. The fiacre rumbled and creaked and banged beneath him, and he stared at the disheartening curve of the driver's slumped, disappointed shoulders. Somerset was both horribly sad and so electric with anticipation that it felt like his body was being fought over by terrible raptors, their beaks made of loneliness and lust, wings beating, their eyes like black suns. Did Aarav make his own way through the city now for their reunion?

How had all this started? With breakfast in a café. And what of Mrs. Baxter and her threats? Had he betrayed England? He didn't care. But – it had cost him nothing, so it had been easy. What would she do? What did she know?

67

To Hell with Mrs. Baxter.

The fiacre driver let him off in front of the cathedral. It was seven-thirty. People littered the street out front – a sign indicated that at 8:30 there would be a musical performance by the famous pianist Witold Kamińska, and following that he would be accompanied by a girl's choir from a nearby convent. Somerset knew he was early, but he looked about for Aarav anyway. He was nowhere to be seen. Somerset gazed down the streets and sidewalks – with every fiacre he saw, he imagined Aarav in it, gleaming like a knight in armor, though he knew Aarav used the tram when he was alone. Somerset was surrounded by conversation, laughter. It was unbearable. The inchoate future tormented him. He would sell his soul for certainty.

He looked at his watch. Only five minutes had passed. He smoked a cigarette, though his throat was dry. It was done all too quick, and he sucked it to its very limits, then cast it into the street. He stepped back from the gutter quickly as he saw an automobile nearly run a carriage off the street. The automobile's horn shrieked, and then the car peeled around the corner. He heard the people around him reacting with surprise, condemnation, and ridicule. What terrible machines, someone was saying, who can stand them? And they were dangerous anyway! There should be a law against them.

Somerset looked at his watch again. Seventeen minutes until eight. He could wait that long. Aarav would be hear soon. God, it was like he could feel Aarav emanating from across the city, the buildings vibrating as the thundering of Aarav's magnificent heart pulsed through them. Ecstatic love, twisted by the voids of despair and fear, broke through his body, his fingers were shaking, he was amazed someone hadn't noticed his condition and called for a doctor. The street lamps flickered; traffic slowed on the street and conversation around him hesitated; a tenuous silence erupted, almost louder than the noise before. He could feel the presence of everyone around him, suspended in a moment of postponement and lack of things to say. Then the traffic picked up, and the din of the city punched through the transient silence.

Down the street, a column of school girls in blue uniforms were approaching the cathedral two by two, led by a *Mère préfète*. They were singing softly, led by the *Mère préfète*, and the harmony seemed to tiptoe in like a surreptitious glance, their voices like resonating bells. The girls looked happy and self-satisfied, smiling to themselves, confident; whatever myriad of little slights, wars, and infatuations they must have lived with every day were forgotten – they were together, their own buttress standing between themselves and the world, adulthood, everything.

At the end of the column, there was a beautiful Indian girl, her hair black and straight as a sure, quick stroke of a fountain pen. She alone seemed to have sadness and disregard in her eyes, yet she sung none the same (or at least mouthed the words.) She had an aquiline nose and full lips, her cheeks high and her neck long; she was taller than the other girls, her back straighter. Yet her arms hung limply at her sides, her feet took reluctant steps.

The girls and the *Mère préfète* filed into the church, and Somerset did not see them again.

Where was Aarav? Somerset peered down the streets. He was shivering now; what had seemed like a warm night earlier now was quite cold. He plunged his hands into his pockets, clutching them into fists, he shuffled from foot to foot, his shoulders ached. He could wait in the cathedral... but then he would not see Aarav approaching. Dejection and gloom filled him until he was bursting; he had to see Aarav again, he just had to!

Up the street, from the opposite direction the choir came, Somerset heard something bumping and clanging, mixed with dissonant, frightened piano tones. Two rough looking men were pushing – shepherding, really – a piano towards the cathedral. The piano was covered with a thick blue blanket that's use seemed more theoretical than practical, and the two workmen were accompanied by a gaunt, wispy-haired man in a black suit who was arguing vehemently with them in Polish. This must have been Witold Kamińska, famous Polish pianist, and he must have thought he was in charge, but the two workmen ignored him, speaking gruffly to each other in French. They were a humorous sight, and when Somerset checked his watch, he realized they were cutting things close – the performance was a short twenty minutes away. The trio reached the cathedral and all three were flabbergasted by the church steps none of them had apparently considered. A priest came out and started pointing around the back of the church to the workmen as Kamińska was even more incensed and theatrical. The workmen nodded, urged the piano to move again, and were followed around back by the ardent pianist.

Where was Aarav? Surely, he should have been here by now. It was almost 8:30, he was late, maybe he had been detained, or the tram was slow. Maybe Aarav was racing here right now, flustered, everything standing between them. Somerset felt a drop of sweat trickle down his back, despite the frigid weather. His stomach spun, delirious with hunger and anxiety. His feet hurt.

The sidewalk was thinning out – people were going into the church or headed off elsewhere. Even the traffic on the street dissipated; the world was perched on the edge of the events of the evening, but Somerset was apart, forlorn, his rendezvous seeming increasingly improbable. If Aarav had been detained, and was *not* coming – don't think it – it didn't mean that all wasn't well. Perhaps Aarav was just exhausted, or roped into something, and Somerset might receive an apology card in the morning, and they would reunite.

Or perhaps Aarav had been arrested.

It was quiet again. He was alone on the street, shivering in the burning golden glow of the street lamps. It was 8:30. The cathedral seemed to stand before him in a frozen moment of a permanent movement, forever reaching for Heaven, but planted down in the Earth, eternally aspiring, but never realizing arrival in its lofty destination. To think – the years, decades, maybe generations it took to build the Cathedral de Saint-Pierre, those men waking every morning to labor on something whose completion they might never see – the cathedral seemed to embody that very idea, in a state of constantly taking flight, but never leaving the ground.

Someone pulled open the doors of the cathedral and music glided out like a votive flock of angels – Somerset recognized Erik Satie's Gnossienne #1, the notes all the more exotic due to their slightly flat notes after the piano's perilous quest to reach the cathedral. The sad,  haunting melody sunk into his skin, then his muscles and organs, until prying its way into his very bones. He was overcome with sorrow. He knew Aarav wasn't coming, that maybe he would never see Aarav again. His heart fell down into his chest, down through his belly and groin, rushing through his legs and down into his feet, until it smashed into the ground, making him lose his balance. His knees went weak, the world around him became excruciating.

The door to the church sealed closed. The melody disappeared. He felt a tap on his shoulder, and hope fluttered explosively. Aarav! At last!

He turned. But it was only Mrs. Baxter – small, beautiful, her expression as cold as the weather. She was dressed in a fur shrug as though she was going to the opera, and her hands were folded together at her waist.

"You!" Exclaimed Somerset. "How?"

She pursed her lips and smiled at him with a sort of annoyed pity. "You are not my only fox in the henhouse, Mr. Maugham."

*

Somerset met Mrs. Baxter at the café once more before he left Geneva. It was on an early evening in mid-December, and cold, very cold. Snow fell outside the café windows, sparkling in the lamp light like tiny, falling suns. Carriages and pedestrians flowed on the street; the city, the world, went on.

"To the best of our knowledge," Mrs. Baxter said, "Chatto and Pradhan escaped Geneva, most probably by boat. Their plan was to obtain a coin die fabricated by a Swiss artisan to counterfeit gold sovereigns in India to destabilize the currency."

Somerset let it sink in. Had that been Aarav's plan all along, his real reason for being in Geneva? Had their sumptuous medley of days spent together all been a distraction, an entertainment to kill time? Is that what occupied Aarav's mind when he had been reticent?

"It's a bit of a scandal for Pradhan's parents. They've been interviewed by the police."

There was more than one India. For Aarav, all of them had become one, a gestalt in his heart and imagination that he would stop at nothing to bring forth from the realm of the ideal into the real world. Aarav had tried to tell him. He hadn't listened.

But they had loved each other. The things they had whispered. The caresses they had shared. Aarav had been distant, yes, but Somerset had revealed his soul. Had Aarav not liked what he saw?

"I am sure you wish you could have been more help," Mrs. Baxter said poisonously. "But officials in India know to look out for the counterfeit coins, so it was all for naught, really. But we have another assignment for you now, in Marseille, something a little more… orderly."

She took a drag from her cigarette. "I wonder, Mr. Maugham, you and Pradhan… were you in love with him? Is that something men like you do?"

Somerset lowered his eyes to his shoes. "Does it matter?"

Mrs. Baxter sighed. "I suppose not. Time does not bless us all with wisdom. Will you be…all right?"

He didn't know the answer to her simple question. What had the whims of history and serendipity done to him? He thought of his first night with Aarav, his warm skin in the carriage in the cool air, their lips moving together in ecstasy, the prelude to their imminent lovemaking. Had every action he had taken, every word he said, every decision he made, really led here, where he had nothing? Had anything changed? He was right back where he started, but now nursing a misery he had not imagined.

"Mr. Maugham? I asked if you are going to be all right."

Somerset looked up at her and formed a smile on his face. "Yes," he told her. "I'll be incredibly fine, darling."

# The Unbearable Faith of Carson McCullers

Winter in Paris could be miserable, and after four days of frigid, unrelenting rain, Carson felt pretty miserable herself. The heating in their flat was shaky, and incessant cold air penetrated the glass of the old windows. The ancient plumbing was erratic, the stove went out at odd times, and the electricity was fickle. And, since the flat was at the top of the building, it was riddled with dripping leaks from a dilapidated roof.

Why had she left New York for this? She knew the answer — for peace and quiet, mainly; for a man, secondly; and — she must not forget — to get away and write.

The war was over, and free Paris was a hesitantly optimistic, supposedly romantic, and cheap place to live. She had to admit, the summer and fall left her exuberant. But now, in the constant pelting rain and cold, she was having second thoughts, and an oozing depression overwhelmed her.

It was January 1947. Carson was 29 years old. Before the war, her first novel, *The Heart is a Lonely Hunter,* was published to great acclaim. Since her success, she indulged in the splendors of literary fame and the high life.

Preceding her visit to France, her novel had been translated into French. Upon her arrival, she was greeted in high esteem by the French literati, including the likes of Jean-Paul Sartre and Simone de Beauvoir; however, since she could not speak French, it was challenging to communicate with them, and her time in Paris proved to be a little lonely.

Carson came at the behest of Reeves McCullers, her on-again, off-again husband of ten years. Reeves was a veteran who had been injured during the war, and he remembered Europe fondly and been eager to return. Carson, who could afford to live anywhere, agreed to satisfy his desires.

On that cold day in January, Carson sat on her sofa with a knit blanket across her lap. She was working on a new story, and as an adamant perfectionist, she wrestled with both ecstasy and terror as the hours dragged. Sentences could torture her — but the joyful prickling up her spine when she found just the right words made it all worthwhile.

At a quarter to three, she heard the front door of the flat unlock. Reeves came in.

"Hello, honey," he said, smiling, wet from the rain as he dropped his umbrella in the corner.

"Hi," she murmured, a grin overtaking her. She was glad to see her husband after the long day; the tedium was over. Reeves carried the day's mail in his hands.

"Any news?" She asked.

"Nothing good," he replied.

"Anything from UNESCO?"

"I'm afraid not, honey."

Reeves had been trying to find work with the U.N. as his career was at a standstill; he hadn't worked since being released from the army, and was on disability due to an injured wrist.

"Well," she announced. "We can only hope."

"That we can, honey," he said, taking off his coat and hanging it on a hook. He came over to the sofa and sat down. "Do you have any plans for this evening?"

"None."

"I met a swell American couple today," he explained. "I was revisiting the *Sacre-Coeur* and saw them. I knew they were from the States because I heard them discussing the Dodgers." He chuckled to himself.

"And then I saw them again when I grabbed a bite at *Café de la Plume Pourpre,* so I introduced myself. They're from Brooklyn. It was so great to talk to someone without muddling through my French. I hope you don't mind, honey, but I invited them to dinner."

"Oh," said Carson, feeling lazy, "I don't know if I am up to it."

"C'mon," he said, "We haven't entertained in ages. I know we have food in the house. You could cook something. We have wine. It will be nice. They were quite cheery."

"I just wanted a quiet night in, my dear," she told him.

"It *will* be a quiet night in," he replied. "Only two guests. And they're very friendly."

"I haven't been feeling social, Reeves."

"Well," he said, kissing her on the cheek. "It's time for that to change."

She consented. "Oh, alright. I think I know what I can make. And we do have that fine Bordeaux."

"Perfect, darling," her husband said, kissing her wrist. "I'm going to take a bath to warm up."

She laughed. "May you be blessed with hot water, my dear."

Reeves smiled at her. "I'll settle for lukewarm at this point," he quipped.

*

Before Carson was born, Carson's mother believed that her first born child would be a famous genius. This was due to her visit to a psychic during her pregnancy, who assured her that her baby was destined for greatness. Carson's mother did not hesitate to relay this information to every relative and friend in their Southern town of Columbus, Georgia. Her conviction did not waver when Carson was born a girl. However, it took some time before the prophecy came to fruition.

Carson (born Lula Carson Smith) did not display her potential until one night when she was eight years old — returning from an outing to the movies, Carson sat at the family's piano and regaled them with the score of the film. She had no prior training on the instrument, and Carson's mother immediately envisioned her daughter's future career as a musical genius. The following day, she signed Carson up for piano lessons with a local piano teacher.

For the next few years, Carson practiced piano relentlessly both before and after school. Her talent was a brilliant light for the family. While she had two younger siblings, she remained the center of her parents' affections. However, Carson was a reticent child, extremely shy and prone to losing herself in thought. When her mother inquired about her quiet moods, Carson replied, "Thinking is fun too, mama."

When Carson was thirteen, her mother found her Mrs. Taylor, a more talented piano teacher than her first. Carson bloomed under Mrs. Taylor's tutelage. Carson also befriended Mrs. Taylor's daughter, Dani, who was a few months her junior. The two became fast friends. Carson and Dani would ride their bicycles around town or spend time at the local equestrian club near Mrs. Taylor's house, where they would ride horses. Carson loved riding.

Carson enjoyed her musical life but realized she was happiest in her imagination, where she would make up stories and characters based on the people around her. With music, she could only dazzle people with the great work of long-departed composers. But with her writing, she could dazzle *herself* with creations of her own making.

*

Carson baked pork chops and fried some potatoes, flavored with parsley and garlic, for their guests. At half-past seven, a knock on the door had Reeves jumping from his seat.

"They're here!" He exclaimed.

Reeves opened the door, and in stepped a smartly dressed American couple. Reeves took their coats. The man was tall, blond, and dressed in an elegant wool suit. The woman had long, dark curly hair and was wearing a shimmering red dress that left her arms and shoulders bare.

"Good evening, my friends," Reeves greeted them. "Charlie, Martha — please let me introduce you to my wife, Carson."

Carson shook Charlie's hand. His eyes were a piercing blue, and he had a friendly smile. Carson turned to Martha, and her heart fluttered — the woman was beautiful, with riveting brown eyes, full lips, and high, rosy cheeks. They shook hands gently. "I'm very pleased to meet you," Carson said, blushing.

"Thank you for inviting us. We've heard so much about you already, Carson," said Charlie. "A real writer! We are very impressed."

"Yes," said Martha. Her voice was both husky and musical. "Reeves bragged all about you!"

Carson laughed, flattered but bashful. "Well," she said. "That was kind of him, but I assure you I am simply just me!"

"C'mon, sit down, you two," said Reeves. "Drinks?"

"Gin and tonic for me," said Charlie, flopping onto the sofa.

"Same for me," chimed Martha as she sat beside him.

Carson excused herself and returned to the kitchen to make her last-minute preparations for dinner. She listened to Reeves and their guests chat through the open door.

"Such dreadful weather," Charlie complained. "I'd rather have snow."

"I'm damp as a duck!" Martha added.

"Well," said Reeves, "Paris weather does take some getting used to. And I haven't been working, so all I have to do *is* get used to it."

"It must be amazing to be married to a great artist," observed Martha.

"Of course," Reeves told her.

Carson could hear the weight in his reply. She knew Reeves hated being known as 'the husband of Carson McCullers.' But she had to admit — it made her proud of herself and her accomplishments. A woman shouldn't have to pity her husband, but she pitied him nonetheless.

She stepped into the living room to save Reeves from his imagined burden.

"Dinner is served, everyone," she announced.

"Wonderful!" Exclaimed Charlie, as he rose from his seat. "I'm famished. What are we having?"

"Pork chops!" Carson replied.

"A good old-fashioned American meal! Bless your hearts," Martha told her. "Charlie is sick of crepes and snails."

"Indeed, I am," Charlie confirmed. "I'm a meat and potatoes man." He affectionately jabbed Martha with his elbow.

"Don't I know it!" She laughed in response.

"Well, this is an old family recipe," said Carson. "So I hope you enjoy it. Plenty of meat and potatoes."

They sat at the table while Reeves poured wine, generously filling all their glasses. Carson brought the meal to the table. She quietly said grace in her head.

"Please, everyone, help yourself, so it doesn't get cold," she offered, her smile bright.

For a few minutes, there was only the sound of silverware scraping the plates, as everyone enjoyed their first bites of food. Carson was an exceptional cook.

"This is delicious," said Charlie. "One hundred percent U.S.A."

"Yes," agreed Martha. "It's a Godsend."

"Thank you," smiled Carson, basking in the glow.

"It must be amazing to be a world-renown writer," said Martha. "I bet you know all sorts of famous people."

"Oh," replied Carson. "Not really. I don't know any movie stars or senators or anyone like that." She laughed nervously, looking to see Reeves' reaction. He was focused on his supper.

"Do you know any other writers?" Martha pressed.

"Well, I'm good friends with Tennessee Williams."

"The playwright?" Asked Charlie. "My goodness."

"He helped me with the play I'm currently writing," explained Carson.

"That's amazing," said Martha. She looked deep into Carson's eyes and smiled. Carson stared and smiled back. Heat flushed into her cheeks; she hadn't met someone who made her feel like this in quite some time.

"Oh, honey," said Reeves. "Tell them your Hemingway story."

"I don't know…" said Carson. "It's a bit salty."

"C'mon, it will be great," Reeves urged.

"Well," said Carson, laying down her fork. Martha and Charlie were enrapt.

"I was in New York last year to see my editor. Afterwards, we went out to eat at a very posh restaurant. My editor, Frank — who knows Hemingway — saw him dining alone. Frank pulled me over there and insisted on introducing me. Hemingway seemed a bit put out to be interrupted during his dinner, but did say that he had read my book and invited us to sit down. Once we dined and had quite a lot to drink, *Ernest* did loosen up quite a bit. Frank excused himself to go home to his wife. I didn't have anywhere to go, so I stayed to have another drink. One drink lead to two, and before we knew it, the restaurant was closing. Hemingway invited me to a bar nearby that he knew."

Carson eyed her guests for a moment to make sure she had their attention.

"It was raining much like tonight, and we were soon soaked. We started walking down the street, but it was apparent Hemingway was a tad drunk, and confused, and didn't remember where the bar was. We crossed the street, and he stepped into a puddle, soiling the bottom of his pant leg. He swore loudly, and I admit I laughed quite hard. It was amusing to see the *Great Writer* taken down a notch."

Charlie and Martha laughed, and Carson basked in their appreciation.

"We continued walking, and he kept shaking his foot as he walked. *Ernest* was so irritated. Suddenly, he tripped when he stepped up the curb on the other side of the street and fell to his knee. This time I didn't laugh. I asked if he needed help. 'I don't need any help!' He bellowed."

Carson took a breath. "Hemingway seemed to blame me for what happened. He yelled at me as he got up, and confessed he had never read my book, that he didn't have time for female nonsense. I told him at least my books weren't just juvenile exercises in cock measuring."

Martha gave out a hoot. "I'll bet he didn't like that!"

"No, he did not!" laughed Carson. "His face turned red, and he gathered himself before spitting out his last words."

Carson got up from the table, put her hands on her hips, and spoke in a low, male voice —

"'Well, McCullers, I'll tell you this. Neither you nor any other bitch *writer* will ever eclipse my work!'"

The guests laughed at her impression. Carson giggled.

"We stood for a moment, our eyes locked. I saw a cab. I hailed it, jumped in, and left him in the rain heaped in the gutter."

Everyone laughed. Carson sat back down.

"I always suspected he was a bore," said Martha.

"Completely," commented Reeves, "and totally overrated."

"That's a story alright," said Charlie, snickering.

*

When Carson attended high school, she was not popular; in fact, most of her classmates considered her downright peculiar. She dressed oddly in long skirts or sometimes trousers. Often, she wore her father's shirts, preferring earth tones to the brighter colors most of the other girls chose to wear. Beyond her wardrobe, she didn't fit in with the social heartbeat of the school. Her fellow students didn't know that she practiced piano before and after school, leaving her too drained for socializing. Carson knew she was an outsider, but didn't know what to do about it — she was just being herself.

Even as an outcast, she had Dani; the girls continued their friendship despite Carson's schedule and unpopularity. They rode horses, discussed boys, and performed for each other. Dani took part in the plays Carson wrote, acting out Carson's imaginings beautifully.

As Carson edged into adulthood, she found herself more and more dependent on Dani, as she wasn't comfortable confiding in her mother. Carson spent all her free time with her friend and relied on her entirely for her emotional wellbeing. She knew this hurt her mother after how close they had been when she was growing up, but what could she do? She was a teenager, and her mother was her mother.

One day after school, the two girls lounged around Mrs. Taylor's back porch, ostensibly doing their homework, drinking sweet tea and giggling.

"So…" asked Dani as she twirled a strand of her long blond hair in her fingers, "Who would you prefer to be your husband — Bach or Beethoven?" It was a common game they played together, deciding between possible mates.

Carson laughed as she looked up from her textbook. "Beethoven, of course. A man of passion."

"Noooo," argued Dani, happy to be distracted from her studies. "Too serious. Too brooding. Bach is playful, beautiful, airy."

"Uh-uh," protested Carson. "Too religious. I need a man who's a heretic."

They laughed together. Carson felt a warmth in her belly. The truth was, she didn't like any boys. She knew she was supposed to, and kept expecting herself to start — but she felt something was missing. She *was* a teen, and she did think about things like kissing, but when she did, Carson thought about kissing Dani. She wondered what it would be like to feel Dani's body close to hers. She had never kissed or been kissed by anyone. Carson knew that she wasn't *supposed* to kiss girls — but that didn't stop her wanting to.

A bee buzzed in from Mrs. Taylor's garden and circled Dani. She swatted at it.

"Shoo, bee!" She said.

Without thinking, Carson stood and clapped her hands at the bee, killing it between her palms.

"Jee-Zus," cried Dani. "Why are you so weird, Lula?"

Carson wiped the dead bee from her hands, cleaning her sticky palms on her trousers. She was suddenly embarrassed.

"Bee stings hurt," she tried to explain.

"I know that! But you didn't have to kill it…"

"I was just trying to protect you," Carson said, sitting back down.

"Well, if you're willing to commit murder for me, how about doing my math homework too?"

Carson snickered but did not reply. She knew in that moment that she was in love with Dani.

*

Carson's Hemingway story was funny. But it wasn't entirely true. All her life, she had a talent of embellishing the truth in order to entertain her audience. She didn't think there was anything wrong with it — after all, she was a storyteller. She *had* had dinner with Hemingway, but it hadn't rained that night, and he didn't fall into the gutter.

After they left the restaurant, Hemingway simply pissed in an alley and hailed a cab, leaving *her* without ceremony. He *was* a bore. That was the truth, but the truth was for her to know.

"Well," said Martha, "I read your book and *loved* it."

"*The Heart is a Lonely Hunter*?" Carson asked.

"Yes. Loved it." Martha smiled, her eyes sparkling. "I was quite taken with the character of Mick and her dreams of making music. You know, I went to Juilliard briefly to study the violin."

"I went to Juilliard too! I studied the piano," Carson replied. "But I didn't finish."

"Why not?" Martha asked.

"I contracted rheumatic fever," Carson sighed. "I went home to recuperate…and I decided I wanted to be a writer more than a concert pianist."

"I didn't last very long, either," Martha told her.

"Why not?" Carson asked.

"Oh…" Martha said, forcing a smile at Charlie, "Life got in the way, I suppose."

"I love music, but it didn't allow me to be as creative as I wanted," Carson explained. "Writing allows that."

Reeves interrupted, knowing the tell-tale signs of his wife's melancholy.

"It looks like everyone has finished with their dinner. What's say we retire to the other room to have a drink and a smoke?"

The four of them left the dishes on the table and took their empty glasses to the other room. Reeves quickly refilled them.

"Put something on, honey," he told Carson, nodding to the gramophone.

Carson put a Count Basie record on, and they sat with their drinks as the music filled the air.

The conversation turned to talk of the war. While French people they knew were pessimistic despite the vanquishing of the Axis, Americans were giddy with optimism.

"Although," Charlie said, "We're going to have to deal with the Russians eventually."

"If they're anywhere as brutal as their literature, it won't be easy," mused Carson.

Reeves laughed. "Unhappy communists are each unhappy in their own way…" he joked.

"Well," Martha pointed out, "Don't you think the world has had enough war for a while?"

Reeves and Charlie shook their heads. Both were veterans.

"Sadly, the world never tires of war completely," said Reeves.

"Damn it, that's enough war talk," said Martha. "Who wants to dance with me?" She stood and swayed her hips.

The men shook their heads again.

"You know I don't dance, dear," said Charlie, smiling knowingly.

Martha grimaced. "Reeves?"

Reeves looked at Carson. "I think I might be too drunk to stand," he laughed.

"Oh, poo!" Martha exhaled. She turned to Carson. "How about a 'girls only' dance then?"

Carson blushed. "Me?"

Martha smiled. "Sure. I'll lead."

Carson stood up feeling dizzy from the wine. Her face was flushed. Martha's beaming smile lured her across the room. As Carson approached, she wasn't sure what to do, so Martha took her hand and pulled her close until their hips almost touched. The room glowed, and Carson felt a quiet buzz in her ears. Martha placed her other hand on Carson's waist.

"C'mon, sweetheart, dance with me!" Martha's smile was infectious. Carson nervously put her free hand on Martha's shoulder, feeling Martha's body heat through her red dress. Urged on by her partner, Carson let herself sway to the music, and her feet gingerly tapped across the floor. Carson laughed. She was delighted.

"That's good, sweetheart, just like that! Feel the music!" Martha giggled.

It had been a long time since Carson had lost herself like this. She felt intoxicated by Martha's movements. As the music crescendoed, Martha pulled Carson closer, and their stomachs met. Carson laid her chin atop Martha's shoulder, and their cheeks brushed each other.

The record ended, and Martha pulled back, leaving Carson feeling the loss of her touch deep into her heart. Martha laughed and clapped; Carson and the men clapped too. Carson felt faint, as though she was about to pass out.

"I must excuse myself to the bathroom," she told them, stepping quickly from the room.

She wished she could have danced with Martha until the end of time.

*

One day in the hot summer of 1932, Carson and Dani lay across Dani's bed in her room. They both breathed shallowly as they waited for the periodic breezed to come in through the window to soothe their hot skin. After a minute of silence passed, talk turned to the opposite sex.

"I don't think I could be naked in front of a boy," said Dani. "It's just too much, and they're too jerky."

"Me neither," agreed Carson. "Sounds horrible."

"I heard kissing could be fun," observed Dani. "I don't know how you're supposed to get good at it without doing it though."

Carson replied as innocently as she could manage. "We could practice," she suggested.

"With whom?" Dani laughed.

"With each other." Carson turned and looked at her friend straight in the eyes.

"That's silly. We're girls!" Dani told her. She laughed again.

"I'm serious!" Carson said. "That way, we would know what we're doing when the time comes, and the boys won't think we're idiots."

Dani was silent, lost in thought. "I guess that does make good sense."

"Exactly," Carson agreed.

They sat up and peered into each other's eyes.

"Well, what do we do?" Asked Dani.

"I think we just do it," Carson said.

"Just like that?"

"I think so."

"Okay…"

They slowly leaned their faces close together. Carson closed her eyes and leaned in. Their lips lightly brushed, and their teeth bumped.

"Ow!" Exclaimed Dani, touching her mouth. "That hurt." She hesitated for a second. "I guess you're right. We do need to practice."

"I think so too," giggled Carson.

"Alright, let's try again."

They leaned in again, slower this time, and their lips met. They kissed.

Dani pulled apart. "I think that worked better, don't you think?"

"Yes," Carson told her, feeling her cheeks go red and her heart race. "Let's try it some more. I want to be really good at it."

They kissed again. Carson moved her lips against Dani's and gently sucked Dani's bottom lip into her own. Her head felt light as they pulled apart.

Dani took a deep breath. "How are we supposed to breathe?"

"I think through our noses."

"This is complicated," Dani complained.

"That's why we need to practice."

"Okay," said Dani. "Let's try again."

They kissed once more. Carson carefully breathed through her nose as their lips moved against each other. She raised her hand and cupped Dani's face. Dani responded by kissing more passionately.

After a few minutes, they pulled back apart. Carson smiled at her friend, and they giggled.

"That *is* pretty fun," said Dani.

"Yes," Carson agreed, breathless. "It is."

*

Carson closed herself in the bathroom. Not daring to glance at her reflection in the mirror, she threw open the window and let the cold rain spatter against her hot face and neck.

*Why am I so weird?* She asked herself.

The rain was torrential outside, windy and frigid. Carson leaned her head back joyously as the rain splashed her face. She felt the neck of her dress get wet. The only thing she could hear was the hammering rain and her heartbeat.

She knew back in the flat, the music was still playing, and Reeves and their guests were laughing and talking. But Carson needed the cold rain to bring her back to herself.

She sighed and closed the bathroom window. She was quite wet. She laughed, remembering her dance with Martha. Her face reddened again, and a giggle caught in her throat. What pleasure it had been. She wondered how long Martha and Charlie would stay in France? She fantasized about becoming great friends with Martha and wasting their days and nights together. Carson could use a friend like that, maybe –

*Maybe what?* She questioned. A hopeful answer came back – *Maybe there's something between us.*

Carson used the toilet and washed her hands. She took a towel and dried her face and neck. She looked at herself in the mirror and could see the longing in her eyes, something she managed to hide most of the time.

She pulled at the doorknob and opened the door. To her surprise, Martha was standing directly outside.

"I have to use the little girl's room," Martha laughed. She put her hand on Carson's shoulder.

Carson laughed too. It was like they shared a secret. After looking down the hall quickly, Carson seized the moment.

She leaned in and kissed Martha on the lips.

It seemed, at first, Martha kissed back. But Martha pulled back with a merciful smile.

"I'm sorry, sweetie, I'm not like that…"

"Ah!" said Carson, hoping to convey nonchalance but instead exuding disappointment. "I'm just being silly! It must be the wine."

Martha smiled, went into the bathroom, and closed the door behind her. Carson made her way back to the living room to Charlie and Reeves.

Carson slowly sank into a chair. Charlie and Reeves chatted about something menial. Carson didn't pay attention. She felt awful.

The toilet flushed, and Martha came walking down the hall. When Charlie saw her, he stood up. "Well, I guess it's about that time, isn't it, my dear?"

"Yes," agreed Martha. "I think so."

"You're leaving so soon?" Reeves asked.

"Yes," said Charlie. "We're headed down to the Mediterranean early tomorrow."

Martha nodded.

A moment later, they all stood at the door, shaking hands.

"Well," said Martha, "It was such a pleasure to meet you both." She cast a smile at Carson. "Good luck with your writing!"

"Maybe we can see you when you get back?" Carson hoped.

"We might not be back for a while, if at all," Charlie answered sadly. "Martha wants to take a ship to Greece."

"I hear the sun is lovely there," Martha explained.

"I hope you enjoy your trip!" Reeves said.

"I'm sure we will," Charlie replied. "Thank you so much for dinner."

"Yes," said Martha. "Thanks so much!" Martha took Carson's hand and shook it. Carson tried to communicate a thousand things, just with her skin.

"Goodbye!" Said Reeves.

"Goodbye!" Charlie replied.

"Bye!" Martha said breezily.

"Bye-bye," Carson muttered.

The door closed softly.

*

The summer of 1932 ended. As the weather cooled down and the routine of school took over, the bliss of summer faded. Carson returned to school, practicing the piano for hours before and after class.

School was tough for Carson, as she was often exhausted. She also harbored the knowledge that she was smarter than the teachers. Students ignored her, especially the boys.

Dani was pursued by most of the young lads at the school – declining more dates than she accepted. On Sunday afternoons, Dani would tell Carson all about these encounters. The two of them would sprawl among the pillows at Carson's or Dani's house and giggle.

Carson tried not to be jealous.

One day, Dani told Carson about her date with a boy called Marv. His attempts to kiss her had gone awry.

"Maybe *he* should have practiced," chuckled Carson.

"With another boy?" Dani burst out in laughter. "Oh, Lord!"

"What did you do?" Carson asked.

"I tried my best!"

"Maybe we're doing something wrong," Carson opined.

"You think so?"

"We only practiced the once…" Carson pointed out.

"That's true."

"Maybe we should practice some more."

"I don't know," said Dani.

"Well," said Carson. "It's scientific."

"I guess you're right," said Dani.

"So…do you want to practice?"

"Okay…but just a little."

They approached each other on the bed and kissed. They had both gotten good at it and knew each other's movements. Their lips brushed and sucked together, as the girls held their eyes closed.

In bliss, Carson raised her hand and cupped Dani's breast. Her friend broke the kiss and pulled away.

"What was that?" Dani asked, upset.

"I don't know," said Carson nervously. "I was just doing what I thought a boy would do."

"That's too much," explained Dani. "I don't think I'd let a boy do that either."

"It's inevitable," argued Carson, trying to dig herself out of the hole she had made for herself.

"That may be so, but that's not something girls should do." Dani ran her hand through her hair and got off the bed. She sat on the window sill.

"I'm sorry," Carson said, hoping to appease her friend.

"It's okay, let's just not do that again," said Dani. She looked out the window and sighed. "Why are you so weird, Lula?"

Carson folded her hands together, trying to regain her confidence. "I don't know. I just am."

Dani smiled. "It's okay. We'll always be friends."

"Yes," agreed Carson. "We always will."

That night Carson lay in her bed going over the afternoon in her head. She had made a mistake with Dani. She had been so foolish to take it a step further – but she had only done what felt right. Things would be different between them now. Carson knew Dani wouldn't ever love her, couldn't ever love her. Carson realized that she was not like other girls. She didn't desire boys and their clumsy touch. She had different urges.

*Someday,* she thought, *I will meet someone. Somebody who will love me for who I really am. She will be beautiful and think I'm beautiful. We will talk about everything and she will know me and I will know her. It will be love. Real love.*

*Someday.*

*

Reeves surveyed the kitchen and sighed. "Let's leave the dishes until tomorrow, shall we? I'm bushed."

"That's fine," said Carson, knowing it would be her that ended up doing them. Her thoughts were stuck on Martha. "I'm tired too."

Carson looked about the apartment. Empty glasses sat on end tables and ash trays were filled. The gramophone was spinning static at the end of the record. She turned it off by lifting the needle. Silence; except for the sound of the rain pelting outside and Reeves' soft footsteps creaking on the floor.

Carson washed and changed into her nightgown. She used the toilet, and brushed her teeth. Climbing into bed, she pulled the covers tightly against herself.

The wind banged against the walls of the building. The sound of the drip-drip of water from the ceiling into a bucket broke the silence. The lights flickered as the electricity struggled. Despite the weight of the blanket, she was cold; she shivered.

Reeves changed into his pajamas as he spoke of their guests. "Charming couple, aren't they? I had a lovely time. I'm glad you made dinner."

Carson didn't reply and turned over so that her back faced him. Reeves went into the bathroom for his nightly rituals. Carson listened as he coughed and blew his nose. When he had finished, he turned out the last lights and came to bed. The springs whined as he lay his weight on the mattress. He sighed, pulling the covers over himself, moving close to her and pressing his pelvis against her rear end.

"I don't..." he began, "I don't suppose you're feeling *affectionate* tonight, honey?"

She sighed. "No."

"Ah," he murmured. He withdrew from her, settling on his side of the bed. As far as she was concerned – he disappeared from this world.

Carson bit her lip to keep from crying. What a fool she had been to act on her infatuation with Martha! She just kept doing this to herself! She felt like such an idiot.

Her stomach turned. *Why am I so weird?*

She curled into a fetal position and struggled to warm herself. The rain continued, hammering on the roof.

*Someday,* she thought, *I will meet someone. Somebody who will love me for who I really am. She will be beautiful and think I'm beautiful. We will talk about everything and she will know me and I will know her. It will be love. Real love.*

*Someday.*

# The Many Lives of Alice Sheldon

Alli is awake. But she decides the day can wait; and she squeezes her eyes shut, willing herself back to sleep. Her husband, Huntington, speaks to her softly across the bed.

"Alli? Alli, breakfast?"

The blind old fool knows she's awake. She blinks her eyes open, knowing feigning sleep is futile. Light streams in through the picture window, illuminating the crisp white bedsheets. Dust and lint hang in the air.

"Alli?" Ting asks again.

She sighs. "I'm awake, Ting."

Alli is old. Not merely getting old, but actually old. She is seventy-seven. Ting is eighty-four. On days like this, exhaustion hits her even before she gets out of bed; it leaves her feeling like she has lived a dozen lifetimes. She stretches, taking a deep breath. The typical aches and pains course through her body.

"I have to go to the bathroom, Alli," Ting urges.

"Of course," she replies, defeated. Alli raises herself from the bed and coughs violently; a lifetime of smoking has taken its toll. She reaches for her glass of water next to the bed and drinks the entire glass dry in an effort to loosen the phlegm lodged in her throat. Sighing again, she gets up and moves around to Ting's side of the bed. She bends at the waist, to protect her aching back, while Ting raises his arms like a toddler wanting to be picked up. She lifts his substantial weight and prickles of pain run down her lower back.

"C'mon, sweetheart," she says, gasping for breath. "I can't lift you by myself. You have to help."

"I *am* helping," he growls petulantly.

"Well – help more."

Together they manage to get Ting up out of bed and into the bathroom, as they do every morning. By the time Ting makes it to the toilet, both are sweating and panting. Once the morning ablutions are complete, Alli musters all her strength again to lift Ting back off the toilet and return him to the bedroom.

Ting's dragging foot causes him to trip on the door jam. The two of them tumble to the floor. Ting lands squarely on top of Alli and takes the wind right out of her. A sharp pain shoots up her right side. She rolls Ting off of her and checks him first for injury. Nothing seems broken; however, his bathrobe has fallen open, and his wrinkled dignity is on display.

Alli chuckles as she covers Ting and gathers herself. Using all of her limited agility, she brings herself into a standing position. A new ache throbs in her right hip, making it hard to balance. Ting grapples to his knees. Alli helps him the rest of the way. After a struggle, they manage to get back to the bed and take a long moment to rest. Another coughing attack strikes Alli; she reaches for her water glass but finds it empty.

"I'll make breakfast now, sweetheart," she tells her husband once her heart stops racing, and she catches her breath.

It is May 18th, 1987.

*

Alice Sheldon, nee Alice Bradley, more commonly known as the science-fiction writer James Tiptree, Jr., was born in Chicago on August 24th, 1915. Her father, Herbert Bradley, a lawyer who led three expeditions into unmapped Central Africa, was exceptionally wealthy. Her dauntless mother, Mary Hastings Bradley, was a socialite and a famous author in her own right, having written travel books and popular fiction (Alli considered her mother's novels vapid as soon as she was old enough to read them.)

When Alli was a child, wealthy adventurers like her parents benefited from the colonial governments of the third world, and the family often traveled to the Congo on safari. Alli tagged along as her mother and father hunted wild beasts, ordered around the African porters, and drank scotch at sunset.

Once Alli hit puberty, things changed. While her parents continued to travel the world, she festered in boarding school. Alli found escape in drawing and painting, desperately wanting to be an artist. Alli's mother had different dreams, insisting her daughter become a debutante. She put a higher value on Alli's social status than her daughter's education.

Alli acquiesced and went to balls, frustrated boys, and filled up her social calendar simply to please her mother. When high school was over, Alli attended Sarah Lawrence College, which trained young ladies in the art of etiquette and how to be good wives. Before Alli finished university, her mother found a suitable husband for her. Alli was married with all the pomp and celebration that was required of someone of her social standing.

The marriage would only last for five years – five long years that Alli would never get back.

*

Alli prepares a plate of scrambled eggs and toast for Ting. She places it on a tray with a no-spill cup of juice. A strange feeling washes over her, one that occurs frequently in the last few days and weeks. She feels *his* presence. Alli turns her head.

It is her alter ego, James Tiptree, Jr. After all, *he* is the one responsible for her literary success.

Alli imagines him leaning lazily against the kitchen's door frame, a burning cigarette dangling from his plump lips. His thick beard and his dark-framed glasses act like a wall protecting his face, preventing his emotions from being seen.

*"What about me?"* She hears him ask. *"I'm hungry too."*

"Hold on, you bastard," she says under her breath. Alli has been "seeing" him a lot lately and figures her exhaustion is playing havoc with her mind.

Alli leaves Tiptree alone in the kitchen and attends to Ting. She hesitates in front of the steep staircase. Once she climbs the tall steps, she celebrates this small achievement. She pulls her chair to Ting's side of the bed, collapsing into it, and spoon-feeds her infirm husband, hoping he doesn't notice her shortness in breath.

He takes a long tug from his cup and sighs.

"I should be taking care of *you,* my dear," he says. "You're the one who's sick."

"I'm not sick," she replies. "Just a bad heart. Had it since my mother took an active role in my love life," she jokes.

"That may be so, but I still want to help you, my love."

She wipes Ting's mouth with a napkin.

"You can't see anything. How can you possibly help me?"

"A minor inconvenience," he tells her.

"I'm fine," she says. "Really." Alli has lied her entire life. This small fabrication is not hard to pull off.

Ting frowns.

Alli feels a tightness in her chest and is silent for a moment.

"Do you remember our pact?"

"Remind me." Ting's memory used to be razor-sharp.

She takes a breath. "We agreed. When we got too old... we'd..."

Ting wrenches his upper lip and becomes cross. "I'm not ready to die yet, Alli!"

Allis gets angry. Ting is selfish; he has the luxury of his life because she takes care of him. Alli is crushed by her responsibilities, they rob her of her strength and her hope. Defeated, she rises from her chair, taking the tray with her.

"I'm going to turn on the radio for you," Alli says, knowing that to try reason with Ting would be useless. "Then I'm going downstairs to write for a while. Okay?"

"Okay," he says grumpily.

On her way to the door, Alli stops at her bureau. She lays the tray carefully on top and pulls open the top left drawer plucking out a weathered envelope. The outside lettering reflects her unsteady handwriting. It is their suicide note – she wrote it more than ten years ago.

"What are you doing, sweetheart?" Ting asks.

"Nothing."

She leaves the letter on the bureau and continues back downstairs.

*

After her divorce, Alli joined the war effort. In 1942, when Congress created the Women's Army Auxiliary Corps (WAAC), Alli jumped at the chance of freedom. She explained to her mother in a brief letter that she was going to help her country. The truth was that Alli was looking for an independent and honest life – in other words, salvation. She fled her recently terminated marriage, an oppressive family, and a life so far without much happiness. The army would be her new start.

Alli felt disappointment immediately. She felt dejected not only by the regimented skirts, which rode up during drills, or by the catcalls, insults, and leers from the men; but by the fact that the work she was doing was demeaning. Her contribution to the war effort was in the kitchen doing dishes; eventually, she was promoted to repairing toilets. It was not the life she had hoped for. Still, army life suited her. She grew to enjoy the monotony of routine, and she became more disciplined. By the time the war in Europe ended, Alli was used to, even liked it – the rigidly structured hours, the drab olive color of her surroundings, and the discipline it all had instilled in her.

After the war, Alli moved to Washington D.C. and found employment working at the Pentagon. She worked in Photo Interpretation. She felt she was genuinely contributing. With the rise of American power, the government and military expanded their intelligence apparatus, and Alli was part of that infrastructure. She was getting paid to turn her keen eyes to the results of high altitude photography and make sense of the images to provide intel.

Her dream was to travel. She hoped to be deployed to Africa or Asia. Instead, she was shipped to Europe, which didn't offer the adventure she wanted. When she arrived, she accosted her commanding officer, Colonel Huntington Sheldon, demanding to know why her requests for assignments had been denied when her male counterparts got their first choice of deployments. Col. Sheldon invited her to dinner at the officers' chateau to discuss her concerns.

"Sometimes the military makes our decisions for us," Sheldon told her over the meal. He was forty-two, tall, dignified, gray-haired and calm. Alli sensed loneliness in his eyes.

"I could be better used elsewhere," she argued, knowing her resume was flawless. The only thing holding back her career was the unchangeable fact that she was female.

"Uncle Sam has other ideas," he explained. "Besides, I reviewed your file and advocated for you to become part of my team. I only have the best working for me, and that most certainly includes you."

Alli was flattered. She was unused to compliments on her skill.

"How's your steak?" Col. Sheldon asked, closing the subject.

"Good." She admitted defeat, taking solace in knowing someone saw her qualifications and judged her on them instead of her beauty. Her curiosity got the better of her.

"How did you become involved in all this?" She asked him.

Sheldon chuckled. "I come from a family of bankers. I'm what you would call the black sheep. I had to find my own life, and the military provided that for me."

Alli nodded and gazed at the rainy gray mist outside the dining hall's windows. "It's dreary here. What do you do for fun?"

"Fun?" He laughed and took a second to consider her question. "I like to read history. And play chess."

"You play chess?"

"Yes. Passionately."

"I play chess, too," Alli told him. It is not something she usually admitted, as most men found the notion of a woman playing chess silly.

"Do you?" Col. Sheldon asked, intrigued. "You know…they have a few chess boards in the lounge next door. Would you care to play?"

A sly smile took hold of Alli's face.

"I would enjoy that very much, sir. I might just surprise you."

"Oh, really?" He smiled broadly.

"I'm pretty good," she boasted.

He raised an eyebrow, and his doubt spurred her on.

"In fact," she wagered. "I believe I could play blindfolded and still win."

He let out a boisterous laugh. "I don't think I can play blindfolded," he admitted.

"Then — just I will."

Col. Sheldon lifted his napkin to his lips and wiped his mouth. He chuckled and gestured towards the lounge. "Shall we? And… no blindfold – this time."

"Yes, of course."

Despite Col. Sheldon being her C.O., and in charge of her daily assignments, Alli considered none of that mattered on the chessboard. There, he was her opponent. She held nothing back in the game and played expertly. When she won, she thanked Col. Sheldon for the game but walked a fine line being the winner and being a demure woman.

"Well," he said after the loss. "Next time, I might *have* to blindfold you, so that I stand a fighting chance."

"I thought to hold back would be an insult to you, sir."

"Indeed, it would have," he grinned. "And you may call me Ting when we're off-duty. May I call you Alice?"

"Okay, Ting," she answered. "But call me Alli – only my mother calls me Alice."

She smiled. There was a warmth in her chest. Alli was delighted she impressed her superior and was glad he was not a man threatened by an intelligent woman.

*

Alli sits in her office, at her typewriter, waiting for the words to flow.

"I've never believed in entropy," she tells Tiptree, looking for a distraction. She imagines Tiptree lounges on the couch beside her desk and speaks to him as if he is real. "The universe doesn't get less complicated. It gets more complicated. Look at life, for example."

Tiptree agrees. "We're just confused by the chaos we think we see. Instead, everything becomes more intricate."

"Exactly," she says.

Alli stares absently at the blank page. She misses her painkillers. She stopped taking them a few years ago because they put her in a euphoric fog, making her unable to care for Ting properly. Without them, her mind is clear – too clear.

"I've been thinking," Tiptree begins. "About birth."

"How so?" Alli asks, curious.

"Well," he says. "Don't you think, when you're a fetus, and the process of birth begins, that everything you know is collapsing, and what's really happening is beyond your conception. You think you are dying."

Alli thinks about it. "I suppose you are correct." She then clarifies. "But you're not dying. You're being born, and everything before was just a prologue."

109

Tiptree continues. "And then," he says, "it would not be farfetched to imagine that our death, at the end of our life, might be somewhat of a birth as well?"

"To what?" She asks.

"Ahhh, now that's the real question," Tiptree finishes.

*

Alli and Ting married in 1945. The new optimism for a world after the war mirrored their confidence in each other. Their ceremony was small, with only their families attending; her mother approved the match once she heard of Ting's family's money. Alli and Ting continued to work closely together in Europe until the government called them back to Washington.

Alli liked being married and being a wife. It gave her much-needed independence from her family, and she felt a real sense of equality with Ting. He was financially secure, thoughtful, and he respected her creativity. But, despite their compatibility, the physical aspect of their love was lacking. Ting was affectionate, albeit awkwardly so. During their lovemaking, he would kiss her like a pecking bird as he wiggled on top of her. Smart as he was, he knew little about a woman's body. Talking to him about it was useless and dangerous, as with most men, his ego was fragile when it came to his sexual prowess. Alli loved Ting a great deal but yearned for a deeper physical connection.

Early in their courtship, Ting confessed he had been married once before. He had three children who were being raised by his parents. Sadly, his ex-wife was committed to a sanitarium after suffering a nervous breakdown and was incapable of caring for them. Ting had to relinquish guardianship to his in-laws as his career did not allow him the luxury of a fixed location to raise the children. Once Alli and Ting were married, Alli insisted on reconnecting the children with their father. She was particularly taken with Peter, Ting's youngest son. Peter had large, inquisitive eyes and was timid – exactly how she imagined Ting had been as a child.

It was hard for Alli to get footing after returning to America and being discharged from the military. She quickly realized that all the strides for women's liberation made during the war had been erased. Men returned to the jobs women had assumed in their absence, and now these same women were expected to be submissive to the returning heroes and slink back to their domestic roles. Women who resisted were ridiculed.

As she and Ting sunk into their own routine of domestic life, Alli wondered how she was going to fill her time. Ting's money provided security, but it also created an imbalance between them that was never there in the service.

After multiple failed attempts, it became clear that Alli could not conceive children. This sad realization crushed her. While she did not know if she would be a good mother, it was something she desperately wanted. Her life was suddenly, incredibly, vacant. She began to nourish the hope that perhaps they could take in Ting's children, and she could raise them as her own. But when she ventured to ask Ting about it, he dismissed the idea.

"They're fine exactly where they are," he told her.

Alli set her sights on a writing career. After a couple attempts at journalism (her articles were considered too feminine to be published), she plunged into fiction. She wanted to write about the plights of women — who they were, what they thought, and how their minds and bodies worked. She submitted her stories to publications; however, they were rejected with notes of criticism that they "were not of interest to the reading public."

Alli lost faith.

In the fifties, Ting took a job with the fledgling CIA, and with his recommendation, she did as well. Ting's career was of a higher, more classified status; Alli got a lower position but still worked in analysis. She dove into the role. The work piled on quickly, but Alli refused to allow the workload to defeat her; needing to meet and exceed the expectations of her job, she sought chemical assistance. Alli started taking speed, Benzedrine specifically. Quickly, she became addicted. Her satisfaction in life came with her focus on work. The drugs also combated her debilitating depression. But every high was accompanied by a devastating crash.

Alli often had suicidal thoughts in her darkest moments – or she wanted a divorce, or she wanted a lover, or she wanted out.

"I want to go back to school," she told Ting one day, after coming out of one of her dark episodes.

They were walking through the park near their house, enjoying a crisp evening. It was October. Brisk gusts blew leaves about their feet.

"Okay," Ting said. "That sounds like a great idea." He didn't ask why. He didn't ask how.

In 1957, at the age of forty-one, Alice Sheldon enrolled as an undergraduate in a psychology program at American University. Surrounded by kids young enough to be her children, she started over.

*

Alli goes into the kitchen and makes Ting an egg salad sandwich. She pours milk into the no-spill cup and repeats the routine from the morning, carrying his lunch upstairs on a tray. Halfway up the stairs, she stops to catch her breath as sweat drips down her forehead.

"Lunchtime!" She announces breathlessly once she reaches the top.

"Ah," says Ting. "My Alli. Never late."

She sees he has managed to get into his armchair. "Always thinking of you, my dear," she replies.

He smiles. "Have you eaten yet?"

"Not yet," she answers. "But I will."

"Alli…"

"I'm not hungry yet!"

"You have to eat."

"I will."

She has not dressed yet either; her blue bathrobe from the morning is still wrapped tightly around her body. She doesn't see the point in getting dressed.

Alli realizes Ting needs a bath.

"Do you want to take a shower now or later?" She asks.

"Only if you take it with me," he jokes.

"C'mon," she says. "You're dirty."

"Maybe a bath instead."

After Ting finishes lunch, Alli picks up the tray and heads back downstairs, glancing once again at the letter on the bureau. Perhaps she will take a bath after Ting takes his.

She expected to die a long time ago. But here she is, still. And if Ting dies, she will be alone. *We must go at the same time,* she thinks to herself. It's the only solution.

Alli climbs the stairs once more. She helps Ting undress as she fills the tub with water. With her assistance, he sinks his big, white veiny body into the bath with a sigh. Alli sits on the toilet and reads a women's magazine as he soaps up.

"It says here miniskirts are coming back," she reads aloud.

"That sounds good to me," says Ting.

"Well – I'm not going to wear one."

"Don't be a spoilsport," he laughs.

"You're blind. How would you even know?"

"Oh, I'd know," he jokes.

After Ting finishes his bath, Alli towels him off, helps him dress, and settles him back into his armchair by the radio. *What a miserable existence.*

She closes herself in the bathroom and runs a fresh bath for herself. After slipping into the steaming water, she lights a forbidden cigarette.

Tiptree coughs before he speaks. "You're going to do it, aren't you? Soon? Maybe even today?"

"I don't know what you're talking about," she tells him.

"You're going to kill yourself and old Huntington in there."

She takes a deep drag from her smoke and exhales it. "I don't know," she says, honestly.

"But, you're thinking about it."

"I am."

"You could live a lot longer, you know."

Alli coughs and puts the cigarette out in the tub "Maybe I don't want to live longer. I'm tired. I've had a good life."

From the outside looking in, she had lived an extraordinary life – from the childhood trips to Africa, to her work for Air Force intelligence, to her life with Ting. She may have had a fraught relationship with her mother, and her life wasn't one happy moment followed by another, but she experienced things most people only dreamed of. Alli traveled the world and saw a lot. On top of that, she's a famous author! She is content for this to be her life; this, and nothing else.

Alli empties the tub and pulls her blue robe back on, exiting the bathroom.

"I smell cigarette smoke," says Ting.

"Must be your imagination," she replies.

*

The early sixties were good for Alli and Ting. They developed an equilibrium and spent most of their time together. After finishing her undergraduate degree, Alli worked towards her doctorate at the university, focusing on visual psychology – she was interested in how the brain processed colors and other visual stimuli.

115

The years passed.

But life took a turn for Alli and Ting at the same time it did for the country. Kennedy was assassinated. Soon, the Vietnam war became an all-encompassing reality. She stared out the windows of her empty classrooms as the students (and professors) protested the war, and the police threw cans of teargas in smoky arcs. After the post-war euphoria of the 1950s, it seemed that the world was now falling apart.

At the same time as the political upheaval, the moon landing and other technological advancements filled Alli's imagination with wonder. She started crafting science fiction stories that explored her ideas and reflected the darkness of humankind.

Similarly, her interest in school and research waned. Her peers and professors became frustrated with her lack of interest in research that could gain grants. She preferred abstractions. She wasn't interested in science for its practical applications, but solely for its revelations, no matter how small or useless they might seem to those writing the checks.

Alli spent more time on her stories. She felt she was on to something. The stories were dark, very dark, with wild concepts and merciless scientific proclamations. Characters came to ill ends, human and alien societies were portrayed as evil menaces, and nothing was sacred or absolute. She was free at last to let her imagination run wild. There were no constraints. She finally found her voice and her freedom.

Alli decided to submit her stories to science fiction magazines. Still aware of the imbalance between the sexes, she needed a *nom de plume*. She knew a female writer would never be accepted into the insular fraternity of science fiction. Besides, she didn't consider "Alice Sheldon" as the person writing these stories; it was someone different, her true identity, unshackled by the ephemera of her history and physical body.

She and Ting spent their evenings floating possibilities. They made up names, perused the phone book for inspiration, but nothing stuck. One day they were grocery shopping when Alli spotted a jar of Tiptree jam.

"Tiptree…" she murmured. "James Tiptree…"

"Junior," added Ting.

"Pardon?"

Ting smiled. "James Tiptree, Junior."

Alli laughed, "Of course. You're right. James Tiptree, Jr." Two little letters enshrined her imaginary writer in a legacy.

That night in her office, Alli went through her new stories. Yes. James Tiptree, Jr. That was it. She had found the perfect alias. The perfect identity.

Alli smiled and imagined a knock on the door. The door swung open, and a vague, dark figure stepped in. Her imagination made him tall, gave him a black beard, and thick glasses that magnified his sad, brown eyes. He wore a flannel shirt and jeans as he sauntered in, a burning cigarette drooping from his lips.

"I'm James Tiptree, Jr.," her creation said in a gruff Midwestern accent. "I believe we have work to do."

"Yes," Alli agreed. "We certainly do."

*

At supper time, Alli finally eats, making steaks and baked potatoes for Ting and herself. It is a meal she used to enjoy, but even though she is hungry, she forces herself to swallow, washing down the food with cold milk. After she cleans up, she sits on the front porch, breathing heavily as she smokes an after-dinner cigarette. The street is quiet. Dusk descends on the neighborhood; the gold color looks as if it fell from the heavens.

Alli is at peace with her decision. She is content knowing the steak will be her last meal, and that this will be her last sunset. She has had enough. She is almost gleeful at the finality.

A little girl comes out of the house across the street, pulling along a small, panting dog on a leash. Her hair is braided into pigtails, and she wears a flowered dress. The dog prances at her feet. The girl speaks to it, but Alli can't hear what she is saying.

Alli never had a dog, and can scarcely remember ever being a little girl. Having no children of her own makes the innocence of children a very distant memory. She watches as the girl and the dog frolic down the sidewalk and around the corner out of sight. Alli feels a tug in her womb, remembering the grief of being barren.

She sighs as the sun sets.

*

Alli wasn't the first woman to take on a male pseudonym to make it in the world of literature – it was a long, established tradition. Like countless women before her, the illusion of maleness allowed her to stop being a "woman" writer, and just be a writer.

Alli sent her stories to magazines under Tiptree's name. While she was again rejected, this time editors offered advice on how to improve her stories – something she had never been given as a female author. She rewrote them, focusing on every criticism. The next time she submitted them, they were accepted, first in small publications, then in major magazines. A small stipend accompanied the publications. She was officially a professional science fiction writer. Or at least, James Tiptree, Jr. was.

Her success was like a fever that took hold of her, and she wrote with more vigor. Slowly, Tiptree became a living being; she answered letters from editors in Tiptree's persona; she sold more stories under his alias; and opened a bank account in Tiptree's name, explaining to the woman at the bank that it was a business and perfectly legal. She picked up copies of the magazines at the store, and James Tiptree's name graced the covers.

She received her first piece of fan mail and wrote back in Tiptree's voice. Bemused, she realized she had finally become free to be herself – by pretending to be someone else.

One of her stories was shortlisted for the Nebula Award, a prestigious honor for science fiction stories. Her fame grew. As she wrote her stories, she also wrote letters, keeping up with not only fans but other authors she admired – always in Tiptree's voice. It came to be that she didn't even think about it anymore; she was Tiptree on her typewriter, and that was that.

When Ting's parents died, he inherited a great deal of money. It enabled Alli to quit her job at the university and dedicate all her time to writing. Her output increased exponentially. One day, while she typed in her office, the doorbell rang. She loathed to disrupt her work, but Ting wasn't home, and the visitor was persistent. She went to the door and answered it.

A young man stood on the porch.

"Yes?" She asked. "What can I do for you?"

"I'm looking for Mr. James Tiptree, Jr.," the young man said. "He's a writer. I believe this is his address. I'm a big fan. Are you his wife?"

"No…" Alli replied in shock. She told him the first lie that came to her. "He moved. A month ago. He doesn't live here anymore."

"I see," said the young man, visibly disappointed. "Do you have his new address?"

"I'm sorry, but I don't," Alli told him. "Wish I did."

"Okay. Thank you, ma'am." He turned and left, his shoulders slumped.

Alli closed the door, her heart racing as she realized she had almost been caught in her lie. She had no idea how the stranger had been able to track her down, but later that same day, she opened a P.O. Box for all of Tiptree's future correspondence. She had underestimated her alter ego's popularity and the veracity of his fans. She would have to be much more careful.

1970 was Tiptree's most productive year. Alli wrote story after story and dazzled the science fiction world. Tiptree became legendary. His elusiveness only added to the intrigue – he was an enigma. From reading Tiptree's stories, fans began to deduce that Tiptree probably had been in the military, maybe even the

CIA; no wonder he was so secretive. Science fiction in those days was a close-knit community, where authors interacted with fans at conventions and other events. Tiptree never attended. There were no photos of him. Alli issued droplets of her history here and there to fans and editors who asked, but never enough to form a full identity; she mentioned growing up in Chicago, having a writer as a mother, and trips to Africa. Despite these hints, there was speculation at one point that Tiptree was Henry Kissinger or JD Salinger in disguise.

For the first time in her life, Alli was truly happy. She had found her calling. Her writing brought her peace, and her marriage with Ting was platonic but satisfying. They looked after each other. Alli was comfortable with the fact that Ting didn't really *know* her. But no one did.

1971 came and went. The writing became physically more demanding. Alli was teeming with creativity; however, she developed arthritis in her right hand, and typing became a painful endeavor. She started taking codeine and other painkillers, refusing to allow the pain to stop her. Tiptree reached the highest peaks of science fiction, winning the Hugo and Nebula awards. He did not appear to accept the awards in person.

As Tiptoe's fame grew, Alli began to feel cracks in the façade. In 1974, the world seemed to be in more trouble than ever, with the Nixon investigation tightening its grasp around the country. Alli believed humanity was doomed, and her writing reflected that, to the insatiable appetite and delight of her fans.

Feminism had also taken hold of the country. Writers such as Ursula K. Le Guin and Joanna Russ were making bold victories in science fiction. While corresponding with these two writers as Tiptree, Alli started to feel she wasn't just betraying them, but herself as well. She wanted to write about women again. She wanted to write about feminism, which both thrilled and frightened her, but she had no voice in the industry. Only Tiptree did.

James Tiptree, Jr. wasn't as much fun as he used to be.

Alli's physical pain continued. She underwent surgery on her thumb for her arthritis. She became addicted to amphetamines again, along with painkillers. Ting wasn't immune to health problems himself. Damage to his vascular nerve was leading to complete blindness.

During this time, Alli's mother suffered a stroke and had one setback after another with her health. As her mother grew frail, Alli felt compassion for her, even forgiveness. She spent what time she could with her mother. It was a slow, agonizing process that dragged on.

Depression and sleeplessness filled Alli's days and nights. Ting did his best, making sure Alli ate and socialized. She would have preferred being more reclusive, but she had to admit it was fun interacting with Ting's friends when they knew nothing of her success as a Tiptree. To them, she was just Ting's melancholic wife. Anonymity was a comfort.

When her mother died, a part of Alli died with her. She went back to Chicago and cleaned out her mother's apartment, an experience that could not be numbed by drugs. When she returned home to Virginia, she was greeted by a letter from one of Tiptree's pen pals. She had been found out —

*Jim,*

*There's a rumor going around your real name is Alice Sheldon. Is this true?*

Alli felt dizzy. She collapsed into a chair. Someone had pieced together evidence from what Tiptree had said about his background with an obituary of Alli's mother and published it in an underground sci-fi journal. Alli was both crushed and relieved. After a long night trying to think of ways to deflect the truth, she instead gave into it. Why fight it? She was too old; she didn't have the strength. The next day, she wrote back, admitting everything in six short words —

*Yes. I'm sorry I deceived you.*

She signed the letter as Alice Sheldon.

The truth caught on like wildfire. Science fiction magazines printed the story. The rabid readers of the science fiction world realized they had been duped. Shock resonated through the industry. Some fans claimed they had been betrayed, while others said they suspected the truth all along. Alli both lost and gained something with the revelation. She was no longer living a lie, but she had enjoyed that lie; she not only was exposed as a fraud but worse, she was revealed as Alice Sheldon.

She finished her first novel, much to the pleasure of her agent, who had been after her for one for years as novels sold better than story collections. The book was released under Tiptree's name, with a note on the cover about her real identity. Alli felt she had managed to cross an enormous bridge. But she could not help but look back and feel something tremendous had been lost.

*

Alli huddles in her office with Tiptree.

"I just can't take it anymore, my friend," she tells him, covering her face with her hands.

"I know. I know that as well as you do."

"They'll say I was depressed, that I was deranged. No one understands that this is *my* life with Ting. I have the last say. I'm doing what's best."

"I know."

"I'm going to have a cigarette. Just one more, and that's it," Alli says.

"Okay."

She lights up, takes a long drag and coughs. Oh, how she loves cigarettes. She deserves one more before the end.

Tiptree gets up and sighs.

"Where are you going?" Alli asks.

"Me? I think I'm going to take a walk around the neighborhood."

"Are you coming back?"

"No… No, I don't think so."

"Well." She takes one last look at him. "Goodbye, James Tiptree, Jr."

"Goodbye, Alice Sheldon."

She imagines the door clicking closed on his way out. When she is done with her cigarette, she looks at the clock. It reads 11:02PM. Ting will soon be asleep.

*

In 1977, Alli was having heart trouble, and Ting was losing his sight rapidly. She wrote, but it was a slow, aimless process. It wasn't the same since she had been exposed. She wrote fewer letters, rarely left the house, and started to look after Ting full time.

One night they lay in bed. Alli sighed, then sighed again. She took Ting's hand in her own.

"Make me a promise," she told him.

"What is it, my dear?"

"That we will die together."

"What do you mean?"

"I don't want to be alone," she murmured.

"I don't think that's up to me," Ting said.

"It *is* up to us," Alli argued. "It can be *our* choice."

"You mean suicide?"

125

"I don't like that word."

"You know what that word means," he said.

"I do. We could do it together. We're getting too old, Ting."

"I'm not ready to die yet, Alli."

"I'm just saying – when we *are* ready."

"I don't know if I'll ever be ready."

"It's inevitable," she told him.

"That is true."

"We shouldn't have to suffer."

"We might not."

"I'm suffering now…" she said softly.

"Alli…"

"Just promise me, Ting."

He pursed his lips.

"We have to agree," she insisted.

"Then, I agree. Eventually. Not now."

She squeezed his hand and said nothing else. Once Ting was asleep, Alli got out of bed and wrote their suicide note. It would sit in the bureau for ten years before it was ever read.

*

Midnight passes. It is May 19th, 1987.

Alli quietly finds the gun in the closet. She examines it to see if it is clean. She loads it with two bullets; that is all she will need.

Ting is deeply asleep.

126

She quickly gazes around and takes stock of their history – the pictures on the walls that captured their lives together, the old tatty afghan she had knitted the year they were married strewn across the armchair, her vanity full of the trinkets Ting had given her over the years. This is it.

Alli turns off Ting's radio, and stands over him, aiming the gun at the center of his forehead. As eternity passes as she argues with herself one final time. At last, she focuses… and squeezes the trigger.

The noise is what she expects, but the gun almost jumps out of her old hands. Ting's head whips back into his pillow, and a spray of blood leaps out of the bullet hole.

Everything goes silent.

Alli feels immediate and complete isolation. Real, physical pain spreads from her heart and steals her breath. She has done it. Ting is gone. She looks to her suicide note on the bureau; it is almost over.

The dark smear over the world gets worse. A sickening ooze slips down Alli's spine; her throat closes. Tears stream down her cheeks.

Now it is just her. This is what it feels like to be utterly alone.

Blood pours out of Ting and soaks his pillow more than she expected. It is horrible. She gets a towel from the bathroom and wraps it around his head to lessen the mess.

Outside the window, the street is dark and silent. Ting is waiting – she has to hurry.

She lays down on the bed, next to her husband, where they have slept for decades. She's scared, but she has to hurry – she must find Ting.

Alli puts the gun to her head and takes Ting's hand in her own, enfolding their fingers. She smiles. She is ready.

She is ready to be born.

# The Black Sorcery of Elena Bulgakova

<u>Part One</u>

I met Mikhail Afanasyevich Bulgakov – my Mishka – in February of 1929. And you may ask – Did I know? Did I know at the time that he would be the great love of my life? Yes! Undoubtedly, yes! I just could not admit it.

Let me tell you how it began.

On a cold winter evening, my husband, the formidable Commander Evgeny Alexandrovich Shilovsky, escorted me to a dinner party at the Moiseenka household. In Moscow, it was common for members of the artistic community to mingle with the military elite as it allowed everyone to keep an eye on everyone else – with all subversive activity making its way back to Stalin's ears.

I enjoyed these social parties as they got me out of the house; however, I was supposed to be glowing and submissive — an exhausting practice. I was an accessory to my husband's rank. Despite the superficiality, I was fond of art and artists and relished the opportunity to flutter in their presence. For every interesting conversation about aesthetics and ideas, there were ten boring discussions of party policy. It was during one of these mind-numbing experiences that my eyes glanced around the room and caught sight of *him*.

I knew Mishka's face, though we had not met. An illustration of his likeness accompanied his sketches when he wrote for the newspapers. He was more handsome in person. But it was his work I loved – he imbued his writing with Russia's souls, and his daily sketch was the first thing I used to turn to when I received the morning newspaper. I read his plays, and I had also read his novel, *The White Guard,* before it was banned for 'distorting historical fact.' So yes, though we had not met, I *knew* Mikhail Bulgakov.

He was standing across the room, conversing with a dreadful woman I had the misfortune of being trapped in a conversation with earlier in the evening. As I made eye contact, he raised his eyebrows and looked in my direction. It felt electric when our eyes met. Had this happened with anyone else, I would have looked away. But neither of us broke the glance. He stared deeply into my eyes and smiled. I could feel blushing in my cheeks, and looked away. When I looked again, he was still staring, nodding absently at the woman with whom he was conversing. But I felt it was me whom he was thinking about.

My husband, who was far more concerned with troop discipline and production supply chains, was no lover of the arts. So when the Commander and I were introduced to Mishka and his wife, he became immediately disinterested when he found out Mishka was a writer.

"It is a pleasure to meet you, Elena Sergeevna," Mishka said as he kissed my hand. His voice was deep, with a bemused melody, and his blue eyes were still as enchanting as when we had stared at each other across the room.

"I am Mikhail Afana…"

"I know who you are," I responded, unable to contain my smile. "Doesn't everyone?"

He beamed at me, chuckling. "I wish that were so."

I was dizzy without a drop of alcohol in my blood. I felt Mishka and I were the only humans on Earth. Mishka politely introduced us to his wife — a bland, flat-chested woman with wide hips and thick, dark eyebrows. She must have sensed the attraction between myself and Mishka, for she scowled *audibly*.

The Commander was eager to be introduced to the next couple.

"Until we meet again, Elena Sergeevna," Mishka said to me with a smile.

Throughout dinner, I was lost in a fever. I barely ate. I drank wine copiously to settle my nerves, but my anxiety only increased. Every time I sneaked a look at Mishka, his eyes locked with mine, and he gave me a grin as though we shared a secret. I became faint and excused myself from the table.

I made my way to the back porch, forgetting to bring my coat. The cold air chilled me in my satin gown, bringing me back to reality. I stood facing the gardens and sighed. It had been so long since I felt something like this, attraction; perhaps it was purely physical, but it felt cosmic. Evgeny never made my pulse quicken, and my palms sweat. I chastised myself for engaging in a silly adolescent fantasy. It was ridiculous! I was married! I had two children!

I hesitated to return to the party. Like an answer to a desperate prayer, I heard the patio door open behind me. I knew it was Mishka before I saw him. Exhilaration, mixed with dread, rushed through me. I turned and saw him standing with my fox fur shrug draped in his hands. I raised my eyebrows in surprise; he simply laughed.

"I thought you might be cold, Elena Sergeevna."

"I am fine," I answered, rubbing my arms for warmth.

As he approached, his feet crunched the snow on the porch. He slipped his arms gently around my back and placed the shrug across my shoulders. His face was centimeters from mine, and I could see the stubble peppering his chin. He smelled gently of cologne — and not the cheap swill that littered the black market; he was the kind of man who cared about his scent.

Mishka took a step back and looked at me.

"My God," he said breathlessly. "You have the black eyes of a sorceress!"

I frowned. "Are you insulting me, Mikhail Afanasyevich?"

"No! Not at all," he protested. "I am… captivated."

A fresh wave of dizziness hit me. I turned to look at the snow, needing a distraction. I could not stand to look into his eyes any longer.

Mishka moved beside me and took in the gardens. He seemed impervious to the chill.

"Your husband, the Commander, seems dignified and noble," he said politely.

"Yes," I agreed. "My husband is quite dignified and noble."

"And I understand you have two children?"

I nodded, shocked that he knew about my private life.

"That is nice," he said softly.

"Yes. Two sons. They are seven and nine. It is very nice." I could barely speak.

"And yet..." Mishka began, "I sense your sadness. Something is lacking... and I cannot bear the thought of such a beautiful woman being sad."

I sighed. Was my unhappiness so apparent? Or was he the only one who could see the real me?

I almost turned to him and collapsed into his arms, sharing all my tightly held secrets; but instead, I tried to speak as indifferently as I could.

"Just simple female nerves, I suppose."

"How do you mean?" he asked.

From the start, I could only be honest with him.

"I live a life without love, Mikhail Afanasyevich." I shivered. "There is no such thing as real, true, everlasting love. No such thing exists."

Mishka scoffed. He took my hand. And once more, I fell into his eyes. They were aglow with passion.

"Whoever told you that?" he asked. "May the despicable liar have his tongue cut out!"

He kissed my hand and made me a promise he would never break. "I will show you that kind of love!"

*

At home, later that night, my husband asked me about Mishka. We had been noticed.

"Where did you disappear to, after dinner, with that *writer*?"

I was used to the Commander's jealousy. If all attention was not on him, he pouted like a toddler.

"I didn't disappear, my dear. I simply needed air."

"And so did Bulgakov it seemed."

"A coincidence, I am sure," I replied. "It must have been the fish."

"So you were with him. What did you two talk about?"

The Commander stared at me intently, as though he were interrogating an underling or a prisoner. He made a point of looking into my eyes only when he was scolding me or instructing me how to do something.

In an attempt to steer the conversation, I mentioned the Commander's hero. "I believe Bulgakov is writing a play on the youth of Stalin."

"Is he? His plays have not been produced for some time." The Commander was gleeful.

"That is the public's misfortune," I replied sharply.

The Commander lit a cigarette. "I hear that Stalin takes a personal interest in Bulgakov's career."

"Does he?" I asked, intrigued.

"If Bulgakov's plays are not produced, I am sure it is Stalin's will."

"Perhaps," I answered.

"Well, I forbid you to see him again."

"I will not see him," I said. "Why would such a man want to see me anyway?"

"You forget your beauty, Elena!"

"I am a mother, Evgeny, not a girl," I told him.

"Yes! I encourage you to remember that!" The Commander retorted.

He said nothing else on the matter, and we went to bed.

*

Mishka would not so easily be deterred.

The following day, I received a note from Mishka asking me to join him for a walk in the park. I did not reply. As a wife, it was my role to obey my husband. Despite my desire for this amazing man, I tried to put the matter out of my mind. Things would stay as they were.

Mishka was determined. A few days later, while the Commander was at his office, Mishka brazenly visited the house. Shocked by his audacity, I had my maid refuse him entry. When she returned, she was blushing and flustered. Mishka had told her he would wait for me… forever, if need be.

Of course, I was flattered.

Mishka revisited the next day. When he realized I would not grant him entry into the house, he left a letter for me. His handwriting was beautiful, intelligent.

> *My Dearest Elena,*
>
> *Since we met, I have thought only of you. Before that moment, I was the greatest fool on Earth. I worshipped the ancient poets and their tributes to beauty, which I now realize are trivial, for these so-called poets never laid their eyes on you.*
>
> *Please let us meet so I can see you again.*
>
> *Mishka.*

My husband found out Mishka visited our home and became enraged. The maid *was* under his employ and was accordingly his spy. The Commander had men watch the house. He insulted my reputation as a wife and a mother. His body shook with rage as he yelled, but he never struck me. The chivalrous notions that had first attracted me to him were intact. However, this slight indiscretion was breaking him.

I, however, was floating on the clouds.

I did not reply to Mishka. I could not. I had my duties. I had my sons.

Mishka was hard to dissuade; he continued to visit the house, leaving notes and small trinkets of his devotion. I did not receive him. I read his notes secretively, then burned them immediately, tears in my eyes.

I refused to leave the house in case I ran into him. I stayed away from the front windows. I loved him, but I was trapped. I could not throw everything away for a man I hardly knew. But, oh, how I wanted to!

Three months passed before Mishka stopped coming to the house and leaving notes. Part of me was relieved.

Part of me was devastated.

I hesitated to go out into Moscow society. I stayed home for a month more, unaware I had slipped into a dark depression. I suffocated day by day, wishing for the doorbell to ring. I feared Mishka had forgotten about me, and moved on to some other Muse. I felt hopeless that I had lost my one chance at happiness.

One morning I woke and told myself it was over. The realization left me heartbroken. I needed to escape the confines of the house, so I went for a walk. It was nice to be outside. But I was despondent.

While I waited at an intersection, a voice called out.

"Elena Sergeevna! I cannot live without you!"

I knew immediately it was Mishka. I turned to the sound of his voice. He stood on the other side of the street, holding a newspaper and looking my way, astonished to see me out of doors. A crowd of Muscovites gaped at us. I was taken aback, and could not breathe. Mishka crossed over to me, disregarding the traffic. There he was, standing directly in front of me. My eyes drowned in his.

"Mikhail Afanasyevich! What are you doing here?" I quickly turned from him, ashamed. "I cannot see you!"

"I missed you so," he said, not answering me. He grasped my hands. Electricity jolted through my arms into my heart.

He smiled. "Would you care to walk with me?" he asked.

I wanted it more than anything. I could not hold back my own smile. "Yes. But only for a little while."

I looked about; the people surrounding us had gone back to their business. It felt so magical. It *was* magic. Divine, prophesied — when I was in his presence, the heavens held their breath. He was a man of passion, of genius, of sublimity. I had dreamt of him often over the past months, and now here he stood, beside me. I could gather him into my arms if I wished, kiss his lips, run my fingers through his hair. He was handsome, brilliant, sensitive, capable of beautiful words and emotions.

And all he wanted was me.

We strolled slowly. It was springtime now, and the sky was a playful blue, with delicate rows of curled white clouds.

"How have you been, Elena Sergeevna?"

"I have been well, Mikhail Afanasyevich." My cheeks burned as I blushed.

"Please," he said. "Call me, Mishka."

I already referred to him that way in my head, as that was how he signed his letters. But I did not reply.

Instead, I took his arm in mine.

*

138

The Commander found out, of course, through his spies, and forbade me again to see Mishka. But I could no longer stay away. I saw Mishka almost every day when my sons were tutored at home. At first, I didn't harbor the thought of leaving the Commander. In fact, I wasn't thinking at all. I just knew I needed to see Mishka.

At home, my husband treated me with shouts or silence, there was no middle ground. I preferred the silence and took to sleeping in another room. Word got around. I was ostracized — the other women in our circle gossiped about me.

My sons weren't quite old enough to know what was going on. Nevertheless, they took my side. Oh, how my children hated their father! He never showed them any love, having procured an heir from his first wife. I also hated my husband! He denied me any sentiment of love. I was a possession to him, an accoutrement, and now I was an embarrassment. I had been wrong to marry at such a young age. But I did have my sons, whom I loved.

I never loved my husband. So, it was not difficult to want to leave him. Did I consider that I would be leaving a life of privilege for a writer who lived in the artists' collective? Of course. Did I care? Let me tell you — a life of love is worth any sacrifice. That was my hope then, and I know now that I was right. Did I care that I could lose everything I had, including my sons? Yes. That was the only thing that made me hesitate, the loss of my children. So, for the moment, I waited.

Inside I seethed. I made the Commander's life a living hell. I knew I couldn't ask him for a divorce — he had to command it. His power and influence were too strong. He could take everything from me. And that I would not allow.

I never understood why the Commander kept me. Out of spite, perhaps. He was stubborn too, and dreaded people talking about him in a derogatory way. He wished it would all go away.

In the meantime, I continued meeting with Mishka. He begged me to leave the Commander. When I could not answer, he would kiss me and weep. I wept too.

I started talking to sympathetic friends about my ordeals. I spread every distasteful truth I could reveal about my husband. He was an honorable man, but no one is entirely flawless, and I had been privy to his complaints about the Party for years. Rumors spread. His career suffered.

It was a dangerous card to play, but when one is in a state of hopelessness, no risk is too great. I was in love.

It all came to a head one night in August of 1932. The Commander and I were having dinner at his superior's home, along with three other couples. The Commander insisted I accompany him, as he was well aware of appearances and refused to allow the dissolution of our marriage to affect his career.

One of the wives, laughing, said, "My darling Elena, I have heard a ragged, lovesick artist has been accosting you on the streets. Surely, he must be driving you mad. Why don't you have your husband shoot him?" All the women joined in her laughter.

"Well," I said to the table, glancing at the Commander. "He is indeed a great artist. And a man of intelligence and conviction. The kind of man I *should* have married."

That night at home, my husband demanded a divorce. I had humiliated him in front of the people who mattered most.

On October 4th, the day after my divorce was finalized, I married Mikhail Bulgakov, surrounded by a small circle of friends and family. The ceremony was simple, but I felt it was the beginning of my real life. During our vows, I looked into Mishka's eyes and knew my love for him was complete. I saw his love for me was returned tenfold. The celebration after was the happiest night of my life; we drank vodka, danced, and laughed without a care in the world. We imagined a future filled with wonder and beauty.

The Commander had granted me care of my children. He didn't care enough about them to use them as a pawn to hurt me, so my sons and I moved into Mishka's flat at the artists' collective. Mishka utterly spoiled my boys, playing with them constantly and teaching them endless songs from the opera on his piano. It was only during these moments that I realized how miserable I was with the Commander — I had never imagined such joy. The accommodations were meager, but Mishka's flat had something that my grand house with the Commander did not — love. We had the necessities, gas heat, and electricity. I found that domestic life with Mishka made our family more than content.

Mishka often described the time before we married as his 'Years of Catastrophe.' We both foolishly believed that the dark times would end now that we were together.

However, we were naïve in thinking that work such as Mishka's, would be successful in Stalin's Russia. The Secret Police watched us constantly. Mishka was still traumatized by their seizure of his work and personal documents years before. There was light — Moscow Theatre was thinking of producing Mishka's play about the youth of Stalin. But Mishka felt the theatre was stringing him along so that they could profit from the controversy of his name. He sensed his play would never be produced.

One night, he returned home from work, and I sensed something was troubling him. After supper, once the boys were asleep, I begged him to tell me what was wrong. He told me he was visited at the theatre by Party officials, who seized all the copies of his play and harassed him for two hours.

He asked, "Do you still write in your diary, my dear Elena?"

"Yes, I do," I admitted. "When I remember."

"I haven't kept a journal since the Party seized all my work. They did not return my personal diaries, and I still get sick to my stomach, knowing they have read my innermost thoughts. But someone must document what is happening to us, for posterity, for the future."

I shared his need to mark this moment in time.

"I ask you, my dear, please record what happens to us, and my work. Hide it where it cannot be found. So that one day, people will know what we had to endure and the persecution we were placed under."

Mishka knew full well that his lack of success wasn't because he did not have talent, but because he would not adhere to the Party line. Fate and history, he said, conspired against us.

"I will write down everything," I promised him. "People will know. We will be remembered. Perhaps it is not too late. Times change. Success awaits us, if not here, then abroad."

His face was ashen. "All I can do is my best," he said, defeated.


Part Two

Mishka was born in Kiev, in May of 1891. He was the firstborn of seven children. His family was not wealthy, but they were comfortable. He had what could be described as a very happy childhood. His father was a prominent theologist, translator, and essayist, who taught Mishka and his siblings to be respectful and openminded about religion. Art was the cornerstone of Mishka's upbringing, and his family had an extensive library of novels. His parents took him and his siblings to plays and the opera often.

Mishka himself possessed a beautiful baritone singing voice, which he exercised regularly. His childhood dream was to be an opera singer and share the stage with the greats. His favorite opera was Gounod's "Faust," about a scholarly man who sells his soul to the Devil; Mishka must have seen it at least forty times during his youth, each time taking something new from the performance. He was even blessed to have seen the famous Fyodor Chaliapin in the role of Mephistopheles. Mishka would often play parts of the opera on the family's piano, using his majestic singing voice to entertain them.

His happy childhood came to an end in 1907, when his father suddenly went blind, the result of malignant nephrosclerosis. After the sudden diagnosis, his papa died, and neither Mishka or his family were ever the same.

It was during the funeral that Mishka had an experience that would change his life. At the viewing, looking upon his father's lifeless body, Mishka realized that the vibrant soul that had been his father had not perished, but merely vanished, leaving the shell of his corpse behind. Mishka was convinced in that moment that the soul *did* exist; our essence transcends our flesh and blood, and is eternal. Mishka had never been religious before, and he wasn't sure if he was religious now, but he knew that his father still persisted, in one form or another — and they would one day reunite.

Mishka's mother found comfort in a family friend and doctor who suggested that Mishka study medicine. Despite his love for music and literature, Mishka decided to be practical — his father's death had made him aware of both the spiritual and material realities of life.

When the Russian Revolution arrived in 1917, Mishka found himself freshly married and unhappily working as a country doctor. He dealt with the usual accidental wounds and aging bodies, but more often found himself treating venereal disease, which was rampant at the time. Mishka missed the wonders of his childhood, and continuously corresponded with his mother and siblings, longing for happier days. He found relief from the mundanity of his work by taking up a pen and writing about his misfortunes, finding solace in creating his own literature.

As the years passed, Mishka realized he had been mistaken in taking up medicine, and promised to dedicate his life to his writing. It would mean leaving the rural town he lived in and returning to civilization — Moscow. Unfortunately, his timing was not ideal; the 1920s were a time of unrest, and the civil war between the Red and White armies burned fiercely.

Mishka believed his talent would save him, and bring light into a dark time of history. He found a job writing sketches for a Moscow newspaper. Here, he honed his craft. His column became popular as he lovingly illustrated the foibles of ordinary Russian people.

The civil war ended, bringing peace to Russia, but at high cost — most of the country was debilitated. Stalin had won. A terrible future was inevitable.

While working at the newspaper, Mishka finished his first novel, *The White Guard.* It became a small sensation — a tale of pre-Revolutionary times that was a hit with his readers. It was only later that he realized such sentiments would get him into trouble with the Party.

Mishka enjoyed literary success. People began speaking favorably about him at social gatherings and in the press. He felt he had found his voice and come into his own. The future was bright.

Sadly, Stalinist Russia spun its web around everything, and soon cast a shadow on Mishka. He garnered the attention of Stalin himself due to the popularity of his work and politically forbidden sentiments. All of a sudden, he was a threat to the regime. The Secret Police spied on him, and his movements were monitored. His novel was banned and described as Anti-Party propaganda.

Stalin's reach was extensive. Critics became harsh. Newspaper reviews of his new play were biting. The Secret Police raided the theatre and his apartment with little provocation; they stole his work and his diaries for evidence of subversion. Mishka was livid and misguided, thinking his fame gave him more stature than it did. He demanded his work and his diaries be returned immediately, but his pleas fell on deaf ears. He started to include more anti-Soviet messages in his work, even though artists he knew were "disappearing." But his sense of justice — and his ego — would not let it go.

His career suffered greatly. Darkness filled his world, and he lost hope.

Until he met me.

*

In April of 1935, Mishka and I were invited to a Spring ball at the U.S. Ambassador's residence. Most of the notable personages of the city were invited; however, Stalin was not in attendance. Neither was the Commander — he was in the Ukraine. We were surprised by the invite, and Mishka guessed that it was an insult to the Party — his novel had just been published in a limited form in America.

We dressed as best as Mishka's pitiful salary could afford; our finery was dated but would pass for the occasion. The embassy sent a gleaming black car to pick us up. The ball was held in

146

the Arbat District, in the large, neoclassical Spaso home where the ambassador lived. The building was decorated opulently for the event — jarring in the climate of a worldwide depression. Tall young birch trees were potted and planted beneath the flickering glow of the chandeliers. Liquor flowed copiously in crystal goblets, musicians played in the spacious ballroom, and the extravagant food seemed never-ending. In addition, animals from the Moscow zoo, such as pheasants, mountain goats, and zebra finches, had been borrowed, and trembled in cages throughout the property. There was even a bear cub on a leash being led through the guests by its trainer.

"This is exactly what is wrong with our country," Mishka scathingly whispered to me. "This disgusting decadence while the people starve!"

I sipped champagne, enjoying the spectacle for what it was. I was concerned for Mishka, who was drinking heavily, and I feared he might say something regretful.

Over four hundred elite guests mingled, amongst them government ministers and Soviet Marshals. No doubt the Secret Police were in attendance, disguised as guests, ushers, and waiters, hoping to pick up on treasonous conversations — they were always on the lookout for Stalin's enemies.

We found a quiet table, next to a window that overlooked a courtyard lit by colored lamps.

"I want to go home," Mishka said, at last, exasperated by playing a role he despised. I understood his annoyance; it was a role I had to play many times on the Commander's arm.

"I know you do, darling," I told him. "But we must stay until others leave, or it will draw attention."

"It's all being noted, every last movement and word here," Mishka muttered. He flicked a tulip petal sitting on the white tablecloth.

"They have more important concerns than ourselves," I reassured him, wishing I had the power to snap my fingers and burn all his enemies to a crisp.

Later in the evening, the orchestra began playing slow American jazz ballads, and I took Mishka's hand.

"Want to dance?"

He frowned.

"Come on," I teased, dragging him up.

A moment later, we were on the dance floor, in each other's arms, slowing swaying to the music.

"Now, isn't this nice?" I asked.

He forced a smile, but I could see the light for me behind his eyes. I leaned my head on his shoulder, and he pressed his face against my hair. If only everything could have been as simple as my love for him.

The hours passed, and the guests remained, consuming every last drop of alcohol and every morsel of food. By dawn, the bear cub had been given champagne, and let loose of its chain, tumbling to and fro, vomiting. Someone opened the birdcages, and the zebra finches fluttered in the air and perched at the tops of the ornate wall fixtures and in the chandeliers.

"I'm going to write about all these devils and their party," Mishka said quietly to me as we finally left in the morning light. "I'll have my revenge."

And he would.

*

Every writer enjoys sharing his or her work with an audience of readers. But as 1936 began, only Mishka and I knew of his new novel. It was our secret. He dictated it to me, and I wrote it all down with my fountain pen. I would read it back to him, and he would request that I make corrections.

"It's wonderful, my darling," I told him, "But I am unsure of the fantastical elements."

Mishka laughed with glee. "There are truths only to be found in the false, my dear Elena! Truths that can be found nowhere else! Only through representation can we see reality as it really is, especially the evil miasma of Soviet Russia."

He called this work his 'theatrical novel.' He gave it the title *The Master and Margarita,* as it featured its title character 'The Master,' a broken writer, and 'Margarita,' a beautiful woman who loves him — inspired by me. It also starred the Devil, and a giant, talking, gun-toting cat named Behemoth.

We worked diligently on the book whenever we could. I had never seen him so passionate about a project. But it needed to remain a secret. I hid the notebooks in the wall. Neither of us mentioned its existence to anyone.

In 1936, Russia was in the middle of The Great Purge. It was a time when Stalin killed anyone even vaguely opposed to his power. Masses of people were arrested, either to be executed or sent to camps. The government invented roving 'gas vans' to asphyxiate the lives of the accused without fuss.

We watched those around us — both friends and enemies — vanish. People who obviously angered the Party, and those who seemed to have done nothing wrong. Mishka was fearful of the manuscript hidden in the wall. One day, the paranoia took complete hold of him, and he retrieved the manuscript and burned it, knowing its mere existence could get us both killed.

I suggested we try to emigrate, but Mishka hung his head.

"I tried," he told me. "I tried before we met. I pestered every official, wrote to Stalin, tried everything. One day I received a phone call from Stalin himself. At first, I was flattered. But I quickly sensed the danger I was in. *'I understand you want to leave the country,'* Stalin said. I realized my survival was at stake. *'No, no,'* I told him. *'I could never leave Russia. I love my country too much.'* He would not let me leave."

Mishka sighed and covered his face.

"I could almost hear his sinister smile on the other end of the phone. *'Good, good,'* he said."

"Then we're trapped here," I whispered.

"Yes," said Mishka. "I'm sorry, my darling."

He embraced me. I clutched him to my chest as a tear fell from my eye.

"This is all my fault," he said into my ear. "I got you into this…"

"No," I told him. "It's not your fault. It's *their* fault. It's *history's* fault."

A few nights later, I woke up exhilarated and shook Mishka awake.

"My love," I said. "I have had the most insane dream!"

"What was it, my dear?" he asked, groggy but fascinated.

"I dreamt I was a witch, flying naked on a broom above Moscow, breaking the windows of buildings with a hammer. And no one could see me — they could only hear the glass shattering and wonder what was happening!"

"I see," he mused, reaching for his glasses. "I see," he said again.

He rose from the bed and pulled on his pants.

"What is it?" I asked. "What are you doing?"

"We are going to write, my dear," he told me. "Your dream has inspired me! Margarita flies tonight, high above the clouds, under the moonlight, tormenting Muscovites with her invisible laughter!"

I giggled, but there was a pit in my belly. "But Mishka," I said. "You burned the book!"

He shook his head, laughing. "Manuscripts cannot be burned, my dear Elena. They exist in the heart. We must just write it again."

Elation rang through me. "I will make tea!"

*

As 1938 arrived, it looked like our fortunes might improve. The boys were growing up. The Moscow Theatre was interested in Mishka's new play about the life of Moliere. Mishka was

151

employed by an opera house; the job filled him with joy at being around the music he so dearly loved. He gained a spring in his step, and he woke up early in the morning, excited about the day ahead of him.

"At last, Elena!" he said to me. "At last!"

Of course, the excitement was short-lived. The Moliere play never saw production. Also, his work at the opera house was only editing other writers' libretti. He was not allowed to write his own.

Despair returned and cast a shadow over our happiness. We survived The Great Purge, but our life was still full of desperation and fear.

Mishka's health was not well. We took a trip to Leningrad to see his family in the hopes that a vacation would lift his spirits. While we were there, Mishka's sight temporarily failed him. Plagued by memories of his father's loss of sight, Mishka rushed to a doctor. It was an extensive wait before he could be examined. He was called into the little door, and I waited outside. When he came out, he was pale and almost collapsed.

"What is it?" I asked, frightened. I took his hand. "Please, tell me what's wrong!"

Mishka did not look me in the eyes and pulled out of my grasp. "I have just received my death sentence!" he cried.

Mishka had been diagnosed with nephrosclerosis, the same ailment that had taken his father at a young age. He was told his immediate future would involve delirium, extreme discomfort, and, ultimately, death.

A terrible cloud hung over us. Mishka became morose and began to forget the simplest things. One day I came home to find him at the piano, trying to remember how to play a melody from his beloved 'Faust.' His fingers wouldn't work at the keys, and awkward, ailing notes whimpered as he tried.

I took his cold hands in mine and kissed his forehead.

"What are we going to do?" he asked me.

"Our best," I told him, as a tear fell from my eye.

"Do you regret leaving your husband?"

"No!" I protested. I wrapped my arms around him. "I will never regret being with you, never!"

"I have only brought you sadness and hardship," he said quietly.

"No!" I promised him. "You have brought me love. Love I never thought I deserved. I would never trade my time with you for anything!"

"We don't have much time left," he whispered.

I felt him shudder as he broke down in tears. I held him as tightly as I could.

"You have given me so much happiness," he breathed into my neck.

I kissed him. "There is such thing as real, true, everlasting love," I whispered, weeping.

I felt Mishka smile against my lips.

"I will show you that kind of love!" I said.

## Part Three

Despite his ailing condition, Mishka invited our close friends over for a reading of *The Master and Margarita*. I argued with him; not only was he unwell, but sharing his work would be dangerous if the Party caught wind of it.

Mishka would not relent. "Give me this, at least, my dear!"

How could I refuse?

We invited four of our closest friends over one evening in the late fall of 1938. I had managed to get my hands on some pork chops, and I served them with the cheap, ill-smelling vodka that we all drank in our communist paradise. Mishka was almost his old self — laughing, debating, discussing literature and the opera. He was lifted by the spirits of our friends.

After dinner, Mishka let our friends know he was going to read from his new work. They eyed me fearfully; thankfully Mishka did not notice. If he had noticed, I knew he felt he had nothing to lose. Stalin had stolen his success, and now he was dying.

Mishka read the opening chapter, where a Party art critic is beheaded with vigor. He continued with scenes where Margarita flies over Moscow and then serves at the Devil's grand ball. After the reading, our friends applauded hesitantly, but I saw the strain on their faces. Each congratulated Mishka politely and made excuses about the hour getting late. One of our friends took me aside and voiced his concerns before leaving.

"Elena," he said, "You must destroy this work."

I pretended I did not understand his concern.

"Mikhail might be dying," he continued, "but such work will put you in danger. You should burn it immediately — for your safety, and the safety of your sons."

I did not know what to say. I knew our friend was right, and I was aware of the danger.

But, if I convinced Mishka to destroy his work, what would be left behind after he died? He believed posterity would redeem him — one day Stalin would die, and the truth could be told.

"Of course," I lied to our friend. "We will burn it tonight."

*

Four slow, agonizing months passed, and Mishka's pain increased. Soon he was nearly bedridden. I took care of his every need. We continued to work on the novel, secretly, which sapped what little strength he had left, but it also gave him a reason to keep fighting. One day, when he was almost completely blind and in agony, he beckoned me over. He took my hands in his, kissed my fingers, and told me he loved me. It sounded very much like a goodbye, and I was not ready to hear it.

"My dear," he whispered. "I need you to help me."

"Anything, Mishka," I told him. "Whatever you need."

"Go to your ex-husband. Ask if he can provide me with a revolver."

"Why?" I asked, already knowing the answer.

"My love," he said to me. "If I have such a tool, I can put myself out of my misery."

"No, Mishka!" I wept.

"Please, my love," he begged me. "Do as I ask."

*

I met the Commander for lunch at a club reserved for military and Party officials. He had become very gray and gained a bit of weight since we divorced. He had lines around his eyes that made him appear tired.

He ordered steaks and fine red wine, and invited me to eat. My palms were clammy, and my breath rapid. There was a pain in the center of my chest.

When I looked at him, he smirked — as if to tell me he knew this moment would come – a moment when I would return to him, regretting my decision to leave him. His grin was self-satisfied, and he chewed his meat while he leered at me. He seemed more petty than I remembered, and my hopes dimmed.

"Now, my Elena," he said once the pleasantries wore off, "Why did you contact me again after all these years?"

I sighed and searched his eyes for mercy. "I have a great favor to ask of you, Evgeny." I knew I was one of the few people who used his first name, and I hoped this sign of intimacy would help soften him to my plea.

He smiled greedily. "What is it, my dear?"

I gathered all my courage. "You see, my husband, Mikhail… he is very sick."

"The great *artist* is sick? How unfortunate," the Commander said, feigning thoughtfulness. "What is wrong?"

"He has nephrosclerosis," I told him. "Hypertension leading to heart failure or cerebral hemorrhage. It's hereditary… his father died of it. He is in a great deal of pain."

I saw a brief moment of compassion in the Commander, maybe as he imagined having the condition himself. His empathy was fleeting.

"And you…" the Commander spoke, "Have been considering your future?"

I realized that he thought I had asked to meet him so that I could beg for forgiveness and be allowed to come back to him.

"No," I said. "The future doesn't exist. The only thing that exists is my husband's pain."

He took a sip of wine, trying not to show his disappointment. "I'm terribly sorry about that, Elena, but I don't know what that could possibly do with me."

"That's where you're wrong," I said. "I have a request of you. You could be of great help to him."

He was nervous. This wasn't going how he had expected. "How?" he asked.

"Like I said… Mikhail is in great pain. I only wish to save him from it."

"I understand that Elena, but I am not a doctor."

"I know," I said. "But you can help. Could you… if you could… get your hands on a gun? A revolver?"

"Whatever for?" he asked.

"So that…" My voice was small. "So that we might end my Mishka's pain."

Now it all became clear to the Commander — why I was here. Not to beg forgiveness. Not to come crawling back to him. He realized I was not coming back — that I would never come back.

His face flushed in anger and disappointment. He chewed his steak disinterestedly, thinking.

"I don't think I can do that," he said at last.

"Why not?"

"Well, it's quite out of the ordinary, not to mention illegal."

"He suffers greatly," I pleaded.

"And why should I help you, Elena? What are you going to do for me?"

I could not look at him.

"That is asking too much," he said, wiping his lips. "And once he shoots himself, the police will investigate. Where will you say you procured the weapon from?"

I hadn't thought of that. "We'll just say we always had it."

"They will not believe you."

"Please, Evgeny."

He shook his head, pleased with his argument. "In addition to that, every firearm in this country is being requisitioned for war. Nothing can be spared. Our country is more important than one man's pain."

I found his patriotism self-serving, as usual.

"We are desperate, Evgeny. If you *ever* cared for me at all, you would do this for me."

"No."

"Please…"

"It is impossible," the Commander said. "I see no reason to help you. That is final."

I began to cry. I didn't want to be vulnerable in front of him, but I couldn't hide my despair. I shuddered as tears fell from my eyes.

"Don't be so melodramatic, Elena. We both know you don't have a heart."

Anger filled me. "I may not have had a heart while we were married," I growled. "Because you sucked it out of me. Yes, I *never* loved you. Who possibly could? You are a cold, soulless excuse for a man."

"Oh please!" he said, raising his voice while the other diners gaped at us. "It's not *my* fault you made a fool of yourself and ruined your life!"

I tried to remain calm. Instead, I slammed my fists on the table and spat in his face.

*

I walked home. And you may ask – did I doubt myself?

Yes. I doubted. But I never regretted leaving the Commander for Mishka. I had thrown away a life of privilege in a starving and oppressed country in exchange for a life of hardship, but I gained more than I lost. I had done it for love, and I did not regret that for one moment.

I doubted. I doubted I had the strength to get through what lay ahead. I doubted I could communicate to Mishka with my eyes that there was nothing to fear. I doubted that I could console him while he suffered unimaginable pain while I endured my own sorrow in losing him. I would be lying if I said I didn't want to flee and find a hole to hide from the immediate future of Mishka's dying days. But I could never do such a thing. I was in it to the end.

I was trapped — I did not blame Mishka, and neither did I blame myself. Did I blame God? I do not know. I did wonder how He could ask me to suffer so much. A desperate landscape lay before me, and I refused to turn back. Mishka would die; I would not. I would be alone while he would be gone. There was no escaping that.

I could only do my best.

*

I rationed what morphine I could procure on the black market to relieve Mishka's pain. His lucid moments became fleeting, and Mishka fell victim to hallucinations. His suffering was tremendous, and he was not entirely himself. He started calling me "Margarita," and speaking of the Devil, whom he announced was coming for him. Mishka talked about his departed mother and father as though they were still alive and in the room with him. He pleaded with God. He begged for mercy.

One day he seemed to be feeling better.

"I want to take a walk outside," he told me.

"It's blistering cold out there, my love," I responded.

"I don't care," he said. "Please, my dear wife, I need to be outside in the fresh air."

I bundled us up, and I helped him out onto the streets of Moscow. He seemed to enjoy the wind on his face, despite the intense chill. It reminded me of the walks we had taken when we first met. Our jaunt was short-lived. He soon told me he was tired and needed to return home. It was his last trip outside.

Sensing the end was imminent, Mishka dictated the last changes to his novel. I carefully made the corrections and read them back to him. When we finished, he let out a great sigh.

"Protect it with your life," he said in his weak voice. "It is my legacy. Its time will come…I know it…"

The days passed slowly.

"I love you, my Margarita," he told me again and again. I always repeated back —

"I love you, my Mishka."

Spring was coming. I refused to leave Mishka's side. Close to his last day, he managed the strength to ask me to kiss him. I did, happily; his lips were cold. The passing hours became excruciating, long, and filled with sadness. He lingered, dying in slow minutes. I had taken to kneeling on the floor next to the bed as I held his hand in mine.

I must have fallen asleep.

When I woke up, my Mishka was gone.

*

The day we buried Mishka was frigid — but Spring was in the air; the birch trees of the city were budding at the tops of their slender trunks, and a hint of hesitant green sprinkled the otherwise resolutely gray Moscow. Other than myself and my two sons, only a few people showed up for the funeral. Not many friends were willing to publicly share in our misery, and I could not judge them too harshly, for I noticed two Secret Policemen photographing and noting those aberrant souls who sympathized with "Mikhail Bulgakov, Subversive."

When they lowered the casket into the Earth, vertigo struck me, and I leaned upon my sons' arms to keep from fainting. The sky went dark, and I imagined the Heavens had been parted by the Devil, come to claim my Mishka at last. I caught my breath, recognized where I was, who I was, and my pain knifed deeper into me.

My sons grieved; Mishka had been more of a father to them than the Commander; they loved him dearly. Mishka had loved them as his own children. After the funeral, though my sons slowly acclimated to their new lives without Mishka, I was left adrift. While I had known this reality would come, I was ill-prepared for it. I didn't know what to do with the seconds, the minutes, the hours, the days.

I spent my time making copies of Mishka's novels and plays, and my personal diaries. I hid the duplicates in the flat walls and floorboards, and I asked my closest friends who believed in Mishka's work to hide copies in their homes as well.

It was torture to go through his writings, to relive their creation, but I was compelled by my despair; it was the only way for me to remain close to him.

Mishka had once said that "manuscripts can't be burned" — they exist in the heart. This is true. But I knew my heart wouldn't last forever, and I was determined that Mishka's work would survive.

Often, I thought of what he had told me of his father's death, how he had realized only a shell had been left of the man that raised him.

I knew that the ineffable, boundless man that I loved had escaped his sorrows at last. His body — and the world — had caged him. And now he flew free.

I was heartbroken.

Epilogue

The war with Germany came and went with my barely noticing, except for the worry for my sons, who served, but not on the front lines — something I had the Commander to thank for, though I imagine he did it out of selfishness rather than compassion.

I endured because I had no choice. There is no pain like grief. You've either known its sharp, clamping jaw — or you have not. The trial of Mishka's passing was nothing to the final, irrevocable loss of him.

He was dead.

*

The years passed.

In the late winter of 1966, there was a knock on my door. My sons had long ago left home, and I lived alone. I had been an old woman for some time. I imagined the knocking was at someone else's door; no one visited me except for my sons. The knocking was insistent, and I realized they were knocking for me.

I climbed off the sofa, where I had been dozing, and made my way to the door. I no longer moved like a young person.

"I'm coming, I'm coming," I grumbled as the knocking persisted. When at last I looked through the peephole, I spied a short, mustached man in a black suit.

"Who is it?" I asked. "What do you want?"

He answered with a question, "Elena Sergeevna Bulgakova?"

"Who is it?" I repeated. He was grating on my nerves.

"My name is Ivan Vladomirovich Popovkin. I am the editor of Moscow Magazine. I'm with the Federation of Writers."

"Yes?" I asked. "How may I help you?"

"I have come about your late husband's work."

I was overcome by dread. Was it the Secret Police?

"There is *no* work. My husband is gone. Leave me alone."

I turned away from the door.

"Elena Sergeevna," he pleaded. "I am a friend, I promise. About your husband's work. What he left behind. If what I have heard is true… I want to publish it!"

And you may ask — was I afraid?

Yes, I was afraid. The Party forgot nothing. Had they come to finish what they had started, all those years ago? Did they plan to take what I had left?

"I told you, there is nothing!" I could feel tears in the corners of my eyes.

"But…" he persisted. "There is *The Master and Margarita*, is there not?"

Hearing the title spoken aloud made me shake.

"Things have changed, Elena Sergeevna! Stalin is long dead. It is a new moment! A moment when great men like your husband can finally be recognized and celebrated!"

They called it "Krushchev's Thaw." The Stalinists had been reportedly ousted. Prisoners had been released from the Gulags. Censorship had been loosened. But…

"How can I trust you?" I asked.

"There are those of us who love your husband's work, Elena Sergeevna. He has become a legend to young writers. Tales of his persecution make us fight for a better Russia."

I looked through the peephole again to appraise him. I saw him take off his hat and run his hand through his balding head of hair.

How many years did I have left on the Earth? Was this the chance I had been waiting for all these years? Had Mishka's dream finally arrived?

"Please!" said Popovkin. "I promise to do right by Mikhail Bulgakov. He was the greatest writer of the Soviet Era!"

I sighed. I let the stranger enter.

*

Two things occurred — *The Master and Margarita* was serialized in Moscow Magazine (though heavily censored); and copies of Mishka's work were smuggled out of the country to be published internationally. Mishka's "Theatrical Novel," became a hit, achieving fame and fans all across Russia. Soon after, an unabridged *Samizdat* — or underground and uncensored publication — found its way into people's hands. It spread across the country. The world of Mishka's imagination had found its way into the minds of millions.

If the Party frowned on this development, they did nothing. I hoped it was because they secretly enjoyed the novel.

I had done it. I had done it for my Mishka.

Magic.

*

And now… here we are. Today. At the end of my story. If only Mishka could have seen this, what he had hoped for and dreamed of. He is finally appreciated. His name will be included next to Pushkin's, Tolstoy's, Dostoevsky's, Gogol's. Mikhail Bulgakov is finally part of the national literature. Part of the pantheon.

Still, the memories of Mishka's torments give me great sorrow. I am saddened that his work is no longer entirely mine — it belongs to everyone. I no longer have his work to protect. It is free. I feel a little lost now that the secret is out.

So, times *have* changed. But what does that do for the past? Nothing. Those that suffered are gone. They cannot be saved by the new present. The world can only change so much, and history happens whether we like it or not — none of us can avoid all of its traps. All we can do is our best.

And if we're lucky — very lucky — we may know real, true, everlasting love.

# The Festering Wound of Stephen King

Stephen was alone for the weekend. He and his wife, Tabitha, had another row and she had taken the kids off to her mother's.

"So long!" he called to her as she pulled out of the driveway.

"You're an asshole!" she had yelled back.

Now that he was alone in the big old house, he decided he would take the opportunity to get totally fucked up. He had four bottles of Jack Daniel's, enough cocaine to deflower an entire busload of nuns, and even five tabs of spectacular LSD. It was, he mused, going to be a perfect weekend.

Stephen was also finishing up his latest novel, "The Bike," about a pair of teenagers who find a bicycle that's a demonic portal to an alternate Earth where nefarious telepathic trees enslave humanity. He was very proud of it. He only had a few chapters left in the beginning of the morning, and as the sun set later that day, he typed the last words of the book, *"The horror comes for us all."*

Now, he told himself, it was time for that Jack Daniel's.

*

It was 1981, and Stephen was the premier horror writer in America. He was rich, famous, and at the height of his skills and talent. While his work wasn't considered "serious" literature, he didn't care. He was being paid to write and he was damn sure going to enjoy it.

A few hours after finishing his book, he was thoroughly wasted on the whiskey and cocaine and listening to Led Zeppelin *really* loud. He felt pretty fucked up, but he could stand to be much more fucked up, so he unwrapped the LSD from its aluminum foil and placed three of the tabs on his tongue. *This is going to be great*, he thought.

At the same time, his belly noisily told him he was hungry. He had not eaten all day. Stephen went to the kitchen and pulled two meat patties out of the freezer. He was going to cook himself some cheeseburgers. Everybody liked cheeseburgers.

He got the frying pan going on the stove and went to the trash can to throw away the paper slips that had covered the patties. He was astonished to find tiny white maggots crawling all over the waste basket. *When was the last time someone took the damn trash out?* he wondered — then remembered it was *his* responsibility.

He opened the basket and pulled the trash out, maggots and all, and tied it up and headed outside to the trash. The October night was cool. Stars looked down on him, and the moon was full. The street was quiet.

Stephen carried the nasty trash out to the garbage can and slammed it in. Then he clapped and wiped his hands on his jeans, hoping to get rid of any stray maggots. As he did so, he felt a terrible presence, and heard a heavy, labored breathing.

*(the horror comes for us all)*

Before he knew it, a giant furred creature slammed into him, and powerful jaws clamped him between his neck and his shoulder.

The beast growled and chewed at him, knocking him onto his back. He lifted his arms to fight off the creature, placing his hands on its large head, trying to push it away as he heard his own screams far in the distance. He dug his fingers into its fur, finding the soft organ of an eye, and in a moment of clarity, stabbed his finger deep into the soft mass.

The beast shrieked and let go of him. He could hear it panting as it ran down the street.

Stephen gasped, trying to catch his breath. The pain was immense. He could feel hot blood all over him and knew he had to get out of the street in case the creature came back, and he struggled to get up. He ran to back to his house, where the Led Zeppelin was still blaring.

The bathroom light flickered as he turned it on, giving him flashes of his pale, wounded countenance. He pulled his shirt off and gaped at the wound — it was impossibly huge, torn flesh ragged, blood racing out of it.

He decided quickly that although he should go to the hospital, his fucked-up state would get him arrested. Besides, the acid hadn't even kicked in yet. *What a mess I've made,* he thought.

Taking a towel to dab and clean the wound, he coughed and then vomited into the sink. So long, Jack Daniel's. When he was done, he collected himself and went back to cleaning the wound. He probably needed to sanitize it. Realizing that would hurt like hell, he decided he would deal with it later.

The fire alarm went off. The burgers! He ran to the kitchen and took the flaming pan off the stove. Well, that was ruined. He wasn't hungry anymore anyway.

He could feel the pain of his wound in every cell of his body, chilling his bones, making his flesh creep, and shaking his fingers. He just needed to rest for a while.

Stephen collapsed in his arm chair and passed out.

*

When he awoke some time later, the wound hurt worse, his chest was caked with blood, and the LSD was *definitely* kicking in. His mind felt enormously wide and spry, his thoughts jumped and frittered, and everything seemed significant.

He went to the bathroom to piss. Afterwards, he examined his wound again. His chest was covered in dried blood. Deep, crimson red fang marks lined his neck and shoulder, dripping yellow pus. The skin around the wound was red and irritated, like a spilled bag of raging pimples.

Stephen stared at his face in the mirror. He was on acid alright. His pupils were huge. He was more concerned though with the writhing hair on his jaw. He could have sworn he had shaved recently, and now he had a half beard. The hair follicles looked like tiny black worms crawling over his skin.

He left the bathroom, shivering. He decided to start a fire in the Ben Franklin stove in his office. This took a while, as he almost forgot how to do it, and he also became distracted with peering at the bark on the logs, which pulsed. Finally, he got the flames going.

The agony of the wound was incessant, but his mind was abuzz enough to forget about it for long moments. He reclined back in his desk chair and picked up his manuscript for "The Bike".

He tried to read it but the words danced. He was suddenly aware that it was five hundred pages of gibberish. Why couldn't he write something about real world stuff? There was such misery across the country, and here he was writing childhood fantasies gone mad. Shouldn't he be doing something that mattered? He was such a disappointment to himself.

In a fury, he decided to burn the manuscript, opening the iron door of the stove and casting the novel into the flames. It burned quickly, flaring up on the bed of the logs. But a when a wind struck the house and went down the chimney, the stove spat out a flaming page that danced around the air of the room. Stephen chased it until it landed on his desk, where he beat it out with a first edition of H.P. Lovecraft's stories — a gift from Tabitha. He looked at the words on the page once the fire was out —

More gibberish!

He gasped, feeling winded and exhausted. He was a wreck. Pivoting his head so he could look at his wound, he found it was bleeding blood and pus again — he must have aggravated it chasing the flaming page.

Stephen went back to the bathroom where he dabbed at the wound with a damp towel. He looked at his reflection again and was bewildered by what he saw — his face was so pale to be almost green, and he could swear his beard had gotten thicker and his eyes had turned black. When he looked closely, he could swear he could see the hair on his chin and cheeks actually slowly growing. He examined his teeth — they looked as though they had grown sharper. The flesh on his face undulated as though the bones underneath were reconfiguring.

Leaving the bathroom for his office again, a heavy weight fell upon his shoulders, and he wondered just what it was that had attacked him. The beast had been too big to be a dog, maybe too big to be a wolf. He remembered its black fur and terrible bloodshot eyes. It had growled and huffed like a monster out of Greek epics.

Maybe it wasn't just a dog or a wolf. Maybe it was... something else.

Stephen began to ruminate on the possibilities, and things quickly added up — the size of the beast, its ferocity, its massive jaw and its unfathomable ferocity — all in congruence with a full moon. An onslaught of abhorrent reality spread through his LSD-riddled brain. Was it so farfetched to think of the creature who had attacked him as something more than science could explain? Had evil legend intruded in Stephen's life in a tragic way?

He was sure of it.

And he knew — then and there — that not only had he been attacked by a werewolf – but soon he would be one too.

*

Dawn arose in harsh metallic gray. Stephen stood on his front porch, watching brown leaves scuttle across the streets. He had thrown a coat with a tall collar upon his back to both warm and cover his wound. He smoked a cigarette while his hand trembled ridiculously. He felt like he was coming down from the acid, and pulled the other two tabs from his pocket, thinking that the LSD was killing the pain. He popped the rest of it into his mouth and sucked the paper into his tongue.

Stephen sadly realized that the only way out of his condition was to destroy himself. It would not be easy. A normal bullet wouldn't do it — he'd just shrug it off. He needed a *silver* bullet. Where would he get that?

He knew that if he did not do this, he would turn into a beast himself, and probably ravage someone as he had been ravage, starting the cycle all over again. That could not be permitted.

He sat on the porch rocker and twitched for a while. When that grew boring, he grabbed a portable radio from the house and flipped it on. The music was soothing. The commercials were insane. He did lines of coke. As he snorted the white powder, his eyes widened, and his nostrils flared. *Yessiree!* he thought to himself. *I'm Stephen King!*

173

When the sun was high enough in the sky, he found his car keys and jumped in the car. It took him a couple minutes to figure it out, but soon he was gliding down the road with the cold air coming through the windows. He was shivering but damn did he feel alive.

Stephen knew there was a Guns and Ammo shop downtown. He knew just where it was, as he had passed it many times. It was probably open now, he thought, and they would be able to help him.

When he arrived, he made sure the parking brake was on, which took a couple minutes, and then he zipped his coat up to cover up his wound. He checked his face in the mirror. He was pale and sickly as fuck, but he also knew gun stores refused business to nobody.

The door rang as he entered. An older man in his sixties was behind the counter. He greeted Stephen.

"Hello, youngster, what can I do for you?"

"I need a gun," Stephen replied.

"Well you've come to the right place. We have plenty. What do you have in mind?"

"Uh, a revolver maybe," Stephen answered.

"We got those," said the old man. "Come over here and take a look." The old man pulled a couple from beneath the counter and placed them on the glass.

Stephen didn't know much about guns. "Which one is easiest?" he asked. "I need one that will just... *do*."

"Well," said the old man. "This one here is simple enough, a woman could use it. Powerful too, and small. Has a nice, but not too strong kick."

"Okay," said Stephen, "I'll take it."

"You're going to need bullets too, I reckon," said the old man. "We got those as well."

"Yeah, definitely," said Stephen. Then he remembered the last detail. "I need silver bullets," he said.

"Silver?" the old man laughed. "I don't think we have any of those."

"You sure?" Stephen asked, desperate. "I need them." His wound itched.

"Don't have 'em," said the old man.

"Do you know where I could get some?"

"They're really not common," the old man replied.

"I just want a straight answer!" Stephen bellowed, surprising himself.

The old man pulled a sawed-off shotgun from behind the counter and pointed it at Stephen. "Here's your straight answer, young fella," he snarled. "I don't know where to get any goddamned silver bullets."

Stephen knew the old man couldn't kill him with the shotgun, but the idea of being shot still seemed a terrible discomfort. "Alright, alright," he said. "I'll just take the revolver and some regular bullets."

"Cash or check?" the old man asked, putting away the shotgun.

*

After he left the Guns and Ammo store with his new revolver, Stephen got back into his car and headed home. Traffic was light, and he managed the car as best he could. Unfortunately, as he made his way on the treelined road back to his house, he started tripping out on the hair on his arms and crashed the car into a ditch.

As he gathered himself afterwards, he felt immensely thankful he had spent five minutes putting on his seatbelt. He unbuckled himself and went to examine the state of the car. It was fucked. Smoke rose out of the hood. And the axle looked broken.

Stephen grabbed his gun and his keys and started walking down the road home. A cold wind blew as the gray sun shone down. He stuck out his thumb as cars passed, but no one stopped. Finally, a station-wagon full of teenagers slowed down and pulled off.

"Thank you, thank you!" Stephen said as he approached. But as he neared, the car raced off and the teens erupted in laughter. Stephen shook his wrist at them and yelled angrily —

"The horror comes for us all, fools!"

He had almost given up when he stuck his thumb out at a small import car coming down the road. The car slowed and stopped next to him, and the passenger door was pushed open.

"Do you need a ride, my son?" asked the forty-ish bearded man inside.

Stephen saw the driver wore a white priest's collar. "I do, sir," he said.

"Well, come on, hop in, we'll get you home," said the priest.

Stephen climbed in and fumbled buckling his seatbelt. The priest drove off and they rode down the street calmly.

"Do you live near?" asked the priest.

"Just down a bit," Stephen answered, nervous. He wondered — was this his last chance at salvation? Should he confess all his sins? Should he confess everything? Was this moment fortuitous? Or an evil omen?

"Red Sox are looking good this year," said the priest, as he turned the sports news on the radio up.

Red Sox? How could the priest talk about sports at a time like this? Couldn't he see how wretched Stephen was, how he stood at the abyss with the devil hounding him?

"Yeah they do," Stephen spoke, almost unable to contain himself from breaking into tears. Would the priest know how to deal with a man suffering from lycanthropy? Who else would? At last, Stephen only said, "It's the next left up here."

"Up there?"

"Yes."

The priest took a left and pulled into the neighborhood.

"It's at the end of the street," said Stephen. "The brown one nestled in the trees."

"I see," said the priest. He pulled in front of Stephen's house. "Here we are!" he announced.

"Thank you, I really appreciate it," said Stephen as he stepped out of the car and shut the door.

*Help me, please!* His mind screamed.

"May God be with you, my son," said the priest, speeding off.

*

As Stephen climbed his porch steps his belly rumbled and he felt enormously hungry. He went to the kitchen and opened the fridge, looking for something to eat. His eyes darted to one of the few things inside — the raw eye-of-round Tabitha had bought to make roast beef. Certain that bloodlust coursed through him, he took out the raw meat and peeled back its cellophane covering, biting into it and chewing the metallic taste into his mouth. He devoured nearly half of it before he quit and laid it on the counter, feeling sick.

It didn't take long before his intestines convulsed like a ten car crash. In less than a moment, he raced to the bathroom and threw himself upon the toilet, having explosive diarrhea and vomiting at the same time. Terror reverberated though him as he guessed his transition into a werewolf was nearing its climax. He sat shivering as his body expelled the last of its humanity.

After it seemed like it had stopped, he managed to stand. He looked at himself in the mirror. Brown blood covered his torso and the wound was red and purple on his neck and shoulder like an alien parasite. In certain areas, his skin had turned black and limpid green. His genitals had shrunk. His beard was thick, his lips were white, his teeth were pink from the blood of the raw meat, and his eyes were red.

*It will begin soon*, he thought, looking at the afternoon light coming through the window. He knew the full moon waited, that night waited, that the beast waited inside his flesh. There was no turning back, no escape, it was inevitable now. He was doomed.

The doorbell rang.

Stephen pulled up his pants and threw his coat back on, zipping it up to the top. Then he peered out the front windows — on the porch out front there were two cops so clean-cut you could set your watch to them. Unable to think of what else to do, he decided to try to play it cool and opened the door.

"Hey officers," he said. "What can I do ya for?"

"Mr. King?"

"Yes?"

"We found your car crashed by the side of Anchor road."

Stephen scratched his beard. "Oh. That. I had a bit of car trouble," he explained.

"How so?"

"Uh, it just died out on me, I guess…"

"There was also an incident at the Guns and Ammo store with you earlier?"

"Oh," started Stephen. "We just had a disagreement."

"Do you still have the gun you purchased, sir?"

He had forgotten about it completely. It was in his coat pocket. "I have it right here in my pocket," he said, reaching for it.

"Sir! Stop what your doing!" shouted the policeman as his compatriot pulled out his gun.

"Uh, okay, sure," Stephen said, stopping his movement.

The cop reached into the coat, retrieving the gun and its ammo. "Have you fired this gun, sir?"

"No."

"Why did you purchase it?"

"Uh, to protect myself." He added, "And other people too."

"How so?"

Stephen thought for a moment. "You wouldn't understand," he muttered finally.

"Sir, you're going to have to come with us."

"But," said Stephen, stepping back. "I haven't done anything wrong. I want to stay here."

Before he knew it, the officer had pinned back his arms and handcuffed him.

"Please, you don't understand! I don't want to hurt anybody!" Stephen whimpered.

"Oh, we understand, sir," the policeman said. He led Stephen out of the house, down the front stairs, towards the police car.

"Please!" Stephen protested. "There isn't time! I'm changing rapidly! It's almost too late! I'm not a violent man!"

The policemen did not reply. They put him in the back of their cruiser. It was a short drive to the police station as Stephen continued to rant, explaining that he was a danger to everyone, and that they must find a cure soon. The world flashed by out the car windows.

He must have blacked out. Suddenly he found himself in a holding cell.

"Please!" he shouted as they locked the door behind him. "You can't do this!"

The police closed the outer door of the holding area and he was alone by himself.

There was a slit of a window in the wall. Late afternoon light crept through it.

*Now what?* he wondered.

Then it dawned on him — he was safe at last! There was no way out of here. When the moon arose, and he turned into a wolf, he wouldn't be able to hurt anyone. He wouldn't be able to escape. The town would be safe from him. He would be safe from himself. He would go through the night in a cage, and then be himself again in the morning.

It was brilliant!

Stephen sat on the bed and smiled. Despite the pain he felt, despite the madness, and fear, and the devouring beast in his blood, he finally felt that something good had happened, and that things weren't so bad after all. Salvation *had* come. He could just lock himself in the jail until the full moon passed, and figure out a cure afterwards. There *had* to be a cure. Hope filled his heart.

Soon, restful, he fell asleep.

*

He woke up when he heard a cop coming into the holding area. He looked at the window — orange light seeped in — it was morning. He was freezing cold but covered in sweat. He had survived the night. He wondered if he had turned; he had no memory of it. What had it been like? Did the cops know what he was now?

"You've been bailed out, King. Time to go," said the cop. He opened the cell. "Come on."

Bailed out? Stephen got up and left the cell. "What?" he asked.

"Your wife's here. Time to go."

His wife? Tabitha! She was here! Elation flooded through him. He followed the officer out of the holding area to where Tabitha was waiting. His happiness evaporated as he saw her angry glare.

"What have you goddamned done now, Steve?" she asked in her mad voice.

"I…" he said, not knowing how to explain.

"For Christ's sake, Steve, what are you doing? You look terrible! We're supposed to be adults," she said, acid in her voice.

"But…" he whispered. Words failed him.

"Let's go, Steve!" She grabbed him by the coat and led him out of the building. "The kids are in the car."

The sun outside was blaring. Tabitha opened the passenger seat of the car and pushed Stephen in, closing the door after him. She got into the driver's seat.

"What's wrong with daddy?" asked one of the kids.

"Daddy's in big trouble," Tabitha replied.

He was so cold. So, so cold. He sat back, clutching the car around him.

"You okay?" Tabitha asked him.

Stephen took a deep breath. "It… it comes for us all," he stuttered, his teeth chattering.

"I'm sure it does," she grunted, pulling out of the police station.

# The Dark Sea of Anna Kavan

1901-1910: France and England

I have the privilege of being both English and rich. It helps that I am also beautiful; however, I must admit my beauty has faded over the years.

Despite these advantages, I was not loved as a child.

I was born Helen Emily Woods, in April of 1901, in Côte d'Azur, France, at a posh resort catering to the English upper crust. My father, Claude Woods, was the owner of a sprawling estate in England — Holeyn Hall, in Wylam, near Newcastle upon Tyne. My mother, Helen Eliza, seventeen years his junior, was the illegitimate granddaughter of a court doctor to Queen Victoria. With no means of supporting herself, she married my father for his money.

My mother was not the nurturing type. Soon after my birth, I was whisked to England under the care of a nurse; my parents remained in France. When I tell people this, they think it strange, shouldn't a mother and father dote on their newborn baby? But I was a necessary inconvenience, both a requisite and result of my parents' marriage — my mother did not love my father, but she had her responsibilities.

When I was reunited with my parents a year later, I received little affection from them. I was under the staff's care and only permitted to visit my mother for ten short minutes daily, directly before dinner. This treatment lasted until I was six, when I was then enrolled in boarding school, deep in the country. You may wonder why my parents sent me so far away. It's simple — my parents were wealthy. That was how it was done.

I don't remember much from my early boarding school years, just cavernous rooms and itchy uniforms; copybooks and the airy chapel. I do remember escaping into my fantasies frequently. I had a fertile imagination, and it allowed me to escape my life's tedium and live any fantasy of my choosing.

My parents did not visit often. I would return home only for the major holidays, such as Christmas and summer break.

My mother was always cold during these sporadic visits. She left me by myself to fill my days as I wanted. I would read or walk the gardens for hours by myself. My father was a little warmer but still distant. He would occasionally ask me about the weather, or if I had enjoyed my lunch. I realize now that this slight modicum of affection made me fall in love with him. I was so starved for any scrap of attention. Our banal conversations tempted me to imagine a future when my father would come to my school grounds and take me away to a new, beautiful life.

I have a distinct memory of being eight or nine years old and returning home to Holeyn Hall for Christmas break. Even though it was winter and dreadfully cold, I spent most of my time wandering the gardens. They seemed magical to me, even with all the flowers sleeping for the winter. With their crystalline ice encasing their branches held up by dark boughs, the bare trees made me think of a fairytale world.

One particularly rainy day kept me from exploring the grounds. Instead, I snuck into my father's library, where I found him sitting at a small table, playing chess with himself. He sat rigidly in his chair, peering intently at the game board, concentrating on his move. Once he committed his game piece, he rose from his chair, walked around to the opposite end of the table, and played the other side. Neither side was favored; both white and black pieces were given the same meticulous attention.

I watched him do this dance twice before he sensed he was not alone. He smiled slightly and spoke without looking directly at me.

"You're not supposed to be in here, little one," he chastised.

I trembled. "I'm sorry."

He looked at me, and his smile widened. "Come here, my dear."

I carefully steps into the room until I stood before him. He looked me up and down.

"You're getting big. Come, sit on daddy's knee."

It was one of his rare moments of affection, and I smiled at the treasure. I could never predict when he would be warm or cold. I lived for these moments.

My father lifted me carefully and sat me on his knee. He smelled strongly of cognac and cigarettes. I looked deeply into his eyes, and he returned my stare.

"Tell me, little one," he said. "Are you enjoying your Christmas holiday?"

"Very much so," I replied, shy.

"I am glad to hear that. Do you like your school?"

"I like it," I lied, eager to please him. I neither cared nor didn't care for it. It was merely a place where I spent my time.

"Your headmistress tells me you like to write stories."

"Yes, I do."

"What kind of stories?"

"I don't know...." I was bashful. I mostly wrote stories about escaping my boarding school with his aid, and I was embarrassed to share this secret.

My father laughed. I wondered if my teachers shared my stories with him; shame rippled down my spine.

He kissed my cheek playfully, and I felt his sharp stubble brush my skin. For a moment, he took my hand and squeezed it gently. An awkward look crossed his face. He released my fingers from his own and eased me off his knee. I was unsteady on my feet.

"Well, run along now, little one." He coughed. "Daddy is busy."

I walked out of the library, feeling confused. Before I left and closed the door behind me, I took one last look at my father as he sipped from his drink and sighed. I pulled the door shut with a click.


1941: Onboard *The Wanderer*


A knocking awakes me from a fitful sleep. I am in my cabin onboard a ship called *The Wanderer.* The vessel is aptly named, as it is indeed wandering — having been refused entry to South Africa, it is now bound for New York. There *is* a war on, I suppose.

I'm lying in a haphazard jumble of limbs — a result, no doubt, from my heavy drinking last night. White light peers through the porthole above my bed, filling the gray box I have been living in for the past weeks with a sickly illumination.

The knock sounds again. Someone is at my door, urgently demanding that I give them my attention. I groan and pull myself out of bed. A headache hits me as I stand. I throw on my dressing gown and tie it quickly around myself as I answer the door. I am greeted by the pale blue eyes of the ship's First Mate.

"Ms. Kavan," he says in his thick Slovak accent, "I am sorry for the inconvenience, but I'm afraid I'm required to confine you to your quarters for the time being."

"Oh?" I ask. "What's happened?"

The First Mate pauses before answering. He is handsome, despite his sharp nose and too thin lips — there is a certain intensity about him.

"Unfortunately," he speaks, "someone fell overboard last night, so we are asking passengers to stay in their cabins while we conduct the search. Standard procedure, you see."

I'm dizzy. Disorientation spirals in my chest. I am suddenly reminded of my father, who "fell" to his death from a steamer's bow on its way to South America when I was only fourteen years old. As the poet W.B. Yeats sang, '*His heart emptied of its mortal dream.*' Everyone, of course, knew it was suicide — my father was morose, despairing, and so…lost.

"Fell overboard?" I ask. "Or jumped?"

"We are searching for her now," the First Mate says, eluding my question."Please stay inside. The crew is busy, and we are only thinking of your safety."

"Do you need any help?"

Why do I ask this? How can I possibly be of help? I reach out to the wall, holding myself up to prevent myself collapsing like an old house.

"No," he says, "you cannot assist us. Thank you."

He looks at me closely and sees that I am distraught. "Are you all right, Ms. Kavan?"

The ship rocks beneath my feet, and I remember there is no ground beneath me, only a vast leviathan.

"Yes," I say, my voice cracking. "Just surprised by the unfortunate news."

"Are you sure?" He asks. "You look unwell."

His chivalry increases my attraction to him. I chide myself for thinking a man can be handsome in a moment like this.

"Yes, quite sure," I say again. "Thank you."

I close the door and fall onto my bed. I hear the First Mate knocking on the next door down.

My mind races. Once the news of my father's death washed back to England, my mother met it with a restrained frown and an appointment with her banker. I was notified in a meeting with my school's headmistress. I had no one to comfort me in my grief. I was not requested at home until the funeral.

I remember lying in my bed at night, imagining my father drowning, all the dark water choking him. I would put my pillow on top of my face and press down with my hands, trying to feel the sensation of my breath being suffocated out of me.

Being stuck in my cabin is the last thing I need right now. Typically, I spend the mornings up on the deck, trying to calm my nerves by watching the sea; the fresh air and the ocean's vastness bring me comfort. Being confined causes a sense of panic in me. Of course, I do have my little bottle of white powder buried deep in my luggage, luminous pleasure just waiting for me.

No. Not now.

I settle for the giant jug of pink gin I have resting on my desk. Moving the short distance from my bed to my chair agitates my headache. I run my fingers over my typewriter and pour a glass of gin. I prepare myself to do some writing.

Another day in paradise.

After my father's death, I was in the absolute care of my mother. What this means is I remained in boarding school. When my schooling came to an end, I was accepted to Oxford, where I wanted to study art. Instead, my mother persuaded me to marry for money — as she had done. I have never been a strong person; if my mother commanded it, I would do it. She controlled the purse strings. She controlled my life.

"We're not as rich as we might appear, my dear," she told me. "We must think about securing your future."

I was living at home. My mother had not remarried — instead, she sampled men as though the world were a buffet. She had momentarily settled on a love interest called Donald Ferguson, a renowned bachelor and administrator of the railroad in Burma, who was five years her junior. Ferguson was a tall, ape-like man with broad shoulders and curly red hair combed slickly across his head. Even freshly shaved, his red hair follicles were visible on his cheeks and neck.

Mother would often invite Ferguson to dinner, where they would laugh boisterously, whisper, then burst into private giggles. I could tell they were talking about me.

"What do you think of Donald?" My mother asked me one day as we sat in the parlor.

"I do not think about him," I replied.

"He comes from good stock," she said. "With an eventual inheritance of no small amount. And he's doing his duty for the Empire in the East."

"What does that have to do with me?" I asked. I was annoyed with her.

"I'm just thinking of your future," said mother. "Donald is looking for a bride."

"Then why don't *you* marry him?" I retorted.

She laughed. "I am an old woman," she said, though she was barely forty. "Donald wants to find a nice young lady who will bear him a brood."

"I am not going to bear him 'a brood,'" I spat at her.

"Do not be so stuck up," my mother scolded. "Donald is perhaps as pleasing a husband as a girl with your temperament can attract."

"I am not marrying him!"

"I hear Burma is quite beautiful," mother said. "Perhaps you could have a pet elephant."

I stormed off to my room.

I did not have any other suitors. While I was beautiful, I was notoriously fickle and had ill spirits. Ferguson wasn't unattractive, but he drank heavily and had a permanent leer in his eyes. I did not want to be married at all, let alone to him; however, I did want to escape my mother and possibly escape England. Mother began to badger me every night, all while Ferguson still visited my mother's bed.

I never fully committed to marrying Ferguson. However, this was a minor detail to my mother, and she started planning the wedding without me. I dreaded the future.

The grim day arrived and was filled with all the pomp required of our social station. I didn't know what Ferguson saw in me, besides my mother's social reputation. During the ceremony, I was overwhelmed by the people watching me. I closed my eyes in terror when we were declared man and wife. As Ferguson bent to kiss me, I felt the room spin. I fixated on the red curly hairs popping out of his tuxedo collar like monkey tails, and felt bile in my throat.

At the reception, I watched as Ferguson gulped down glass after glass of champagne. I became fearful of the evening's requirements, knowing Ferguson would demand we consummate our marriage. I was extremely sheltered, and I knew nothing about sex. Everything I did know I had learned through rumor and my own wild, uninformed suspicions.

Once the guests left, I panicked. My mother kissed me on the cheek and smiled.

"Goodnight, lovebirds!" She said, cradling Ferguson's cheek fondly.

Ferguson led me to our marriage suite. I trembled in my organza dress. Once the doors were closed, he pulled me close to him and started kissing me like a flapping fish; his lips were wet and sloppy, and he tasted of booze. I slapped him across the face.

"Don't be so dramatic, darling," he laughed, pushing me down onto the bed.

His inebriation left his reactions slow, allowing me time to jump up and lock myself in the bathroom. Ferguson, in a rage, bashed the door down as I screamed for help.

No one came.

I stopped fighting and just wished it all away. I wished it would stop, and eventually it did.

While Ferguson lay drunkenly asleep, I crept from the bed and snuck out into the gardens, as I had when I was a child. It was spring. Half-naked, with bloodstains on my silk slip, I sunk my bare toes into the grass and cried.

The roses were wine-dark in the moonlight. This place had been so magical when I was a child.

Where was that magic now?

1941 - Onboard *The Wanderer*

After a few hours in my cramped cabin, I am notified that passengers can move freely about the ship again.

I go up to the dining hall to get breakfast; the room is crowded, as everyone is hungry from being cooped up for the morning.

I sit alone, eat the insipid eggs, chew the tough fried ham, and drench two slices of toast in yellow margarine.

After breakfast, I stand on the deck, gazing out at the ocean, remembering the lost passenger and my father's death. I always imagined my pain unique — but perhaps it was a long tradition, jumping from a ship's bow. My grief is not so unusual, after all. There is a certain romantic element in being swallowed up by the sea's vastness. I peek over the railing and watch the waves lick the ship. I shiver; it is cold.

I need a drink.

I find the First Mate sitting alone in the bar. I surmise that after a night of hard work, he is relaxing after his shift. It is too early for the crowd of passengers to make demands on the bartender, but not for me. The bartender winks in my direction as I am no stranger here. The First Mate sees me and nods. I sit next to him and order a hot toddy.

"Off work?" I ask.

"For now," he smiles, draining his drink and asking for another.

The silence makes us both uncomfortable.

"I'm Novak," he says.

"Anna," I respond.

Novak is tall and  lean, making a perfect arc as he drapes over the bar.

"Where are you headed?" He asks absentmindedly.

"New York, I think."

"You don't sound too sure...."

"I'm *not* sure," I answer.

"I know that feeling." He reflects. "What brings you on our boat in the first place?"

"It's for my health," I tell him, which is mostly true.

"Is it working?"

My fingers tremble. "Nope!"

Novak raises an eyebrow but does not press further.

"I like the sea," he says, changing the subject. He sucks his teeth after taking a sip of his liquor, savoring the taste.

"It's all right," I say.

I sense Novak is a little tight, but who am I to judge?

"A beautiful woman, unaccompanied on a ship…" Novak smiles, his eyes glow.

I chuckle, amused by the flattery.

"Surely, there's a reason you're not married," he observes.

"Surely, there is," I say. Novak makes me feel confident. "You could accompany me."

He laughs but says no more. I have called his bluff. A minute of silence passes.

"Tell me what happened last night," I say.

"Oh! That! Bad business, I'm afraid. Very sad indeed. A young lady leaped to her death."

"Suicide?"

"It looks that way." He frowns. "She left a note for her father — her traveling companion. He is devastated."

"That is very tragic," I agree. My confidence evaporates now that I am reminded of my father. A pit opens in my chest. "Did you find her?"

"No," he says. "We found out too late. The father woke at sunrise. She was gone. The note was left on her pillow."

"How can you tell she jumped?"

"We searched the ship. She is gone."

"I see."

I finish my drink. I feel like I'm going to be sick. I think of the girl. And the father — what despair!

"Are you okay, Anna?" Novak asks sincerely.

"Yes!" I smile forcefully. "Wonderful."

We look at each other. There *is* an attraction of some sort, I can feel it. But I hesitate; despite his unmistakable masculinity, there's something else I can sense, and I wonder for a moment if he prefers the company of men. I decide to put him to the test.

"Are you going to invite me back to your cabin?"

"No," he says.

"Why not?"

He smiles to himself. "Are you going to invite me to yours?"

I think about it. Now I do not know what to think of Novak.

"Perhaps later." I go back to my drink.


1919-1922: Burma


After the disastrous "honeymoon" at a hotel in London, I parted from Ferguson for a short time; he was expected back in Burma. I had a week of respite before I followed him by steamer. The ship, called the *Water Flower*, was like a prisoner's cell before his execution. I felt constantly claustrophobic, even on the upper deck. I dreaded my arrival in an unknown country to a husband I despised. As Yeats sang, '*I was a swan drifting on a dark flood*'. I had traveled abroad with my mother and father, but now I was alone, with only fears for the future. I anticipated further outrage and horror and had no hope.

Did I consider throwing myself off the bow, ending it all? Yes, I did.

The ship arrived in Burma at night. The only person waiting for me was Ferguson's chauffeur, a short Burmese man in a black suit and cap, smelling of cheap tobacco.

"Ship late," he said in broken English. "Mr. Ferguson wait at home for Mrs. Ferguson."

He escorted me to a limousine.

I stared out of the darkened windows as we zoomed past the black city, illuminated only by gas lamps. We passed into the country. The car headlights — which seemed to draw the automobile through the night like pale horses — lit up the yellow flowers of the padauk trees that lined the road, burning their curious color into my memory.

Once we arrived at Ferguson's home, I noticed it was less than ample. In the limited light, it looked sickly, and the grounds seemed uncared for.

I was welcomed by a small staff of servants who informed me their master was asleep. They led me to my prepared room. I collapsed onto the bed, exhausted and full of despair.

I awoke the next morning to gray skies and torrential rain. Ferguson was having lunch when I walked into the dining room.

"My apologies, darling," he told me. "I wanted to meet you, but your ship arrived so late, and my work tires me completely. Come, have something to eat."

I detested him.

After the long trip, I ate ravenously and was profuse in my gratitude towards the servants.

Ferguson became annoyed.

"You don't have to be so polite to the Burmese, darling," he said.

"I'm just thankful for them," I replied. "It was a difficult trip."

"I'm sorry, darling, but it's just *not* done."

That night, he took me to dinner at a nearby hotel where the English congregated in the evenings.It seemed to be the center of the British Empire in Burma and filled with people who could only find money and power by working abroad. The guests greeted me suspiciously, but for what reason, I could not tell. I supposed I was an outsider and would be accepted in time. They all sweated through their clothes in the humidity and drank copious amounts of gin.

As the night drew on, Ferguson became belligerently drunk and threw out decorum by grabbing me salaciously. He laughed when I became embarrassed, while the Englishmen and ladies whispered to each other. I was humiliated in front of the very people I wanted to impress. My frustration with

Ferguson only incensed him. When we made it home, I suffered further outrage similar to my wedding night and honeymoon experience. I hated him.

He was dismissive when he was sober, and a tyrant when he was drunk. He offered me little in either state.

The months passed slowly, in a fever of anxiety and discomfort. During the day while Ferguson worked, or was away on trips, I found solace in the house, despite being incredibly isolated. I did not go out. The other English expatriates did not extend invitations; I deduced they considered Ferguson an apostate, hated by all, and that many of his outings were actually visits to Burmese brothels and gambling houses. When I became too friendly with certain servants, Ferguson fired them. He took glee in isolating me from any comfort. I was utterly alone.

In those days and weeks of seclusion, I armed myself with a fountain pen my father had gifted me years ago, and I began to write again. Basic notes on my feelings gave way to autobiographical stories of my torments. The peace in the house allowed me to escape into my imagination. It became my only joy.

During the rainy season, the heat continued unabated, and despite the vigilance of the servants, rats got inside the house. The Burmese attempted to poison them or beat them with pots and pans. One of the few times I laughed during my stay was when Ferguson broke a tennis racket while trying to bash a rat that was stuck behind the bathroom cistern.

Sometimes, after the rain had slowed, I would gaze out the windows at the distant mountains. They sat like giant, inky emeralds resting under the hot sky. I imagined myself traveling the space between the mansion and the mountains at impossible speed, and the triumph of standing on top of them, feeling powerful and free.

Soon my worst nightmare occurred — I was pregnant. I did not want a baby, and certainly not Ferguson's. I had never known such anguish. I knew it was the inevitable result of Ferguson's outrages upon me. I had no interest in being a mother, and certainly not in a union built upon hate and disgust. I was alone, distraught, trapped, and afraid.

Confronted by the inevitabilities that lay before me, I requested a bath and locked the door behind me. Using one of Ferguson's razors, I opened the veins on my wrists and waited for oblivion.

To my grave disappointment, I was not successful.


1941: Onboard *The Wanderer*


After I leave the bar, I walk along the ship's promenade. A cold wind blows the salty spray from the sea into my face. Above me, the sun is a hazy white splotch in the gray sky. Far away, the round curve of the horizon seems to answer nothing.

The ship undulates. I imagine the slate-colored ocean as a stoic face hiding an incomprehensible mind underneath — vast, tempestuous, horrifying. There is nothing as large on the Earth as the sea, and nothing as beautiful or treacherous. And here I am, floating upon it on a vessel that could be torn to bits or sunk in an instant — if the sea desires it.

A strong wave hits *The Wanderer*, and I have to reset my feet. I hear people further down the deck, chatting amongst themselves. I am crippled by loneliness.

If only things had been different.

I look down at the ship's stern, and see the captain speaking with a gray-haired man who is hunched in a chair looking out to sea. The gentleman seems indifferent to the captain's attention. The captain pats the man gently on the shoulder and leaves him in his hunched state. As the captain passes by me, his eyes are distracted, but he smiles reassuringly and politely nods.

I watch the older gentleman looking out to sea. He seems despondent. His uncombed hair flutters in the wind. His face is ashen, almost green, a stark contrast to the other passengers whose skin is pink from the cold.

The man is clad in a black coat and holds his hands clenched in his lap. I realize I was wrong when I perceived him as hunched; it is more like he is sinking with a great weight on his shoulders. At first, it looks like he is mouthing words or speaking to himself, but upon closer inspection, I notice his lips are trembling; in fact, his whole body is shaking. It's not the cold, I know it's grief, because I have known the feeling myself.

I think about approaching him, but what could I offer in the way of comfort? I'm aware of a twisted symmetry that connects him and I — a daughter who lost her father to the sea, and a father who lost his daughter the same way. How could I explain that to him? He thinks he is alone with his misery. He is not.

I think again of my own father. It's not the despair and hopelessness that I don't understand, but that final leap, that final decision to *actually* do it. I have never had the determination to leap from the bow of a ship. Oh, I have slit my wrists, I have overdosed on barbiturates, but I have never sacrificed myself to the waves like my father did, with no hope of mercy. I suppose where we differed is I still *hoped*, no matter how slightly or obliquely; my father, however — and this man's daughter — must have considered mercy the greatest enemy, something that must be avoided at all cost. Hope was a poison that only prolonged their suffering. They refused its false clemency.

I wish I could tell you I have never understood my father's suicide, but I know that would be a lie. I cannot explain why he did it, but I do *know* why he did it. I know that despair, that feeling of being trapped, that darkness in the heart that suffocates all the light. What I don't accept — and what I don't forgive — is his abandonment of me. I blame that abandonment for almost everything that has gone wrong in my life. I loved him.

He should have loved me.

1922-1925: England and France

After the scandal of my suicide attempt, Ferguson gladly accepted a divorce. I had humiliated him. The incident caused his superiors to take a closer look at his behavior, and he was forced to take responsibility.

He was demoted.

I returned to England to have the baby. While I was not happy to be back under my mother's thumb, I was delighted to be free of Ferguson and Burma.

The months passed without incident. When it came time for the birth, it was difficult — arduous, disgusting, and embarrassing. The midwife lay the child in my arms. I felt crushed by the weight; I had never seen anything so helpless. The midwife instructed me on how to nurse the baby. It all felt so foreign as I held the pink creature to my breast and experienced the odd sensation as it pulled from my breast and swallowed. I stared down at it, hoping to feel a connection. Instead, I saw the baby had a glaze of the same red hair as Ferguson. I shivered and shrieked and pushed the baby back to the midwife.

"Take it away!" I screamed. "I never want to see it again!"

The midwife frowned. "But miss..." she said. "The baby needs to nurse."

How could I be expected to love such a thing? To be reminded of the horrors that brought it into being? Ferguson had broken me. He took what he wanted and left me destroyed. If I had any maternal instincts, they were gone once I saw the red hair. I never even wanted to be married to Ferguson, let alone have his baby. I didn't want to be a mother. All of it filled me with terror.

"No!" I screamed again. "Take it away!"

The midwife nodded slowly and took the baby from the room.

Later that day, my mother visited me. A servant moved a chair next to the bed, and my mother sat upright and stiff.

"Thank you, Marianne," she said, dismissing the servant. "That will be all."

The servant left the room, closing the door behind her.

"Helen, my dear," my mother began, "it's perfectly understandable — I was never one for nursing either. Ghastly business. There are other avenues for feeding your child."

I turned away from my mother and faced the wall. I said nothing. I hated her.

"It is pleasant you had a son, though, don't you think?" My mother asked. "Have you considered what you are going to name him?"

I responded with silence. All of this was my mother's fault. She forced me to marry Ferguson, go to Burma, have the damn baby. She did not care about me.

"I have always liked the name William," she prattled on. "It was your grandfather's name. I thought perhaps it would be a good, strong name for your son."

What did a name matter? All I wished was for the whole world to disappear, and me with it.

"That settles it," my mother said with satisfaction, getting up from her chair. "William, it is."

I had to escape. You might think I should have felt differently, especially after the loveless childhood I had experienced. Shouldn't I have given my son the love I never received? Right a past wrong? I couldn't, that wasn't me, it couldn't ever have been me. I was a monster. My son was better off without me. And I knew I was better off without him. Like me, he would be raised by servants. Like me, he would go to boarding school at a young age. I don't ask for your forgiveness. I'm just telling you the way it was.

Shortly after my body recovered from the birth, I fled England for the south of France, leaving my son behind. It was sunny there, unlike the gray, damp haze of England. I began to heal. I met artistic people like myself and adopted a carefree lifestyle. A bohemian attitude and hedonism spread across Europe — a reaction to the war that had just ended. It seems embarrassing to me now when I remember how silly we were in our artistic ideals and sexual liaisons. At the time, it was a desperate antidote to the poisons of modern civilization.

It was during this time that I first met Orla — Orla Bohannon, daughter of an Irish coal baron. She was beyond rich, beyond clever, and became the first true, dear friend in my life.

I rented a small flat in Cannes and spent most of my time in cafés and restaurants or relaxing at Orla's villa. I was afire with literary ideas, having read André Breton's *Surrealist Manifesto*, and while I dreamt of painting, I knew my paint would have to be made of words and my brush would have to be a pen.

Orla and I visited Paris but mostly lounged around the coastal villages, drinking, sunning ourselves, and teasing the men who came our way. I felt truly alive for the first time in my life. That isn't to say I didn't have bouts of despair; I did, but I felt freer than I ever had before.

I would occasionally visit my mother and son in England, more out of obligation than anything else. The entire time, all I thought about was returning to the sun and sea, and my friends who understood me.

I should have known it couldn't last. Orla's father demanded that she come back to Ireland and marry, or he would cease funding her bohemian lifestyle. We had one final week together, and she promised to go out with a bang. Orla borrowed a car, and we drove down the coast with her poodle in the back, the wind streaming in our hair, the world laid at our feet. But like all happiness, it was fleeting, and we returned to Cannes for one last party.

We drank heavily during the day at the villa. Her brother had come to see her back to Ireland. He was handsome, but gaunt, with that look common to wealthy men who can do whatever they want. I was attracted to him, but Orla told me he was queer.

After a drunken afternoon, the melancholy of Orla's impending departure set in. The rest of the guests left for dinner, leaving Orla and myself alone with her brother, who promised a special surprise to cap off the day and quell our sadness.

He disappeared into his room, while Orla and I waited on the couch, laughing. When he returned, he carried an ornate oriental box the size of a large book.

"What is that?" Orla asked.

"Pandora's box," he chuckled.

He sat cross-legged on the floor before us and opened the box. Inside a velvet pouch was a vial of white powder, and a leather case containing a syringe. I knew what it was from our bohemian friends who used such substances, but I had never tried it myself. Orla and I looked into each other's eyes, elated with surprise.

"Orla," he said, "be a dear and light me a candle, will you?"

And there, in Orla's villa, while the golden orange rays of the sunset came in through the windows, rivulets of cigarette hung over us like gray silk, and a Stravinsky ballet played on the phonograph, I finally fell in love.

With heroin.


## 1941: Onboard *The Wanderer*

After another night of fitful sleep, I find myself exhausted in the morning. Needing some company, I look for Novak in the bar again. I find him as I left him, arched over the bar, drinking Irish whiskey.

"Hello," I say.

"Hello, Anna," he grins shyly.

"Just waking up?" I ask.

"Heading to bed, actually," he answers.

"Ah. Bed."

"How are you today?"

"Onboard a miserable ship," I tell him.

"Is it that bad?"

"It's that good," I laugh.

"You've been on the water a long time," he observes.

"How can you tell?"

"I know my passengers. What are you fleeing from?"

"Everything…" I confess.

"But mostly…?"

"Myself."

"I see."

"I'm addicted to heroin," I admit, astonishing myself with my candor. I need someone to talk to, someone to sympathize with me. To understand me.

Novak grimaces. "And by sailing, you cut off your supply."

"Yes."

"How's that working?"

"Not bad. I conserve."

He places his hand on my shoulder reassuringly.

"I understand. I'm fleeing a wicked addiction myself."

"Oh? What is it?" My inquisitiveness makes me bold.

He sighs. "Perhaps I will tell you sometime."

I'm disappointed; however, the hope of a future secret tickles me. Once again, I wonder if he may be queer.

"We're a sorry lot, aren't we?" I ask.

"No," he says. "Just human."

"All the good things in life are wretched."

"I'll drink to that." He lifts his glass.

Someone enters the door to the bar, and wind from outside blows the hair around my face. Novak reaches over and brushes it from my cheek.

"Thank you," I tell him. He is gentle.

"My pleasure."

"Are you going to invite me to your cabin now?" I press.

He chuckles. "I'm building the anticipation."

"Well, don't keep a girl in suspense forever."

"Maybe next time," he says.

"All right," I grin. "I'll hold you to it."

"Look…" he says, gesturing with his head to the window.

The older gentleman I had observed sitting in the wind yesterday is passing outside on the deck.

"Is that the father of the girl who threw herself overboard?" I ask Novak.

"Yes."

"I was watching him yesterday. I suspected it was him. He looks ruined."

"Yes, he does," Novak says. "He just watches the sea, all day."

"My father killed himself by jumping from a ship's bow," I tell him quietly. "I was fourteen." I'm not sure why I share this with Novak. Again, I need sympathy.

Novak stares at me. I cannot meet his gaze.

"I'm sorry," he says. "Then, this must remind you."

"It does."

He finishes his drink quickly. "I'm tired," he says. "But I promise — next time we can meet in private."

"Tomorrow?" I ask, hopefully.

"Tomorrow," he promises.

I leave my drink on the bar and exit. Outside, it is blistery and cold. I find the old gentleman sitting in a deck chair, his eyes trained on the sea. I can see by his body language that he is truly broken. I bite my lip and approach him. I tell myself I know his pain.

"Hello," I say, as kindly as I can.

He does not reply or acknowledge my presence in any way. His light blue eyes barely flicker with life as he stares absently at the ocean.

"I'm sorry about your daughter," I tell him quietly. "I hope she is at peace now."

Instantly I feel foolish issuing such platitudes. I remember people saying the same banal things when my father died. What the hell did they know?

I feel compelled to speak to this man, to make a connection.

"I'm sure she knew you loved her very much," I continue, wondering if I believed this about my father.

Such trite condolences; why am I bothering him? I think I know him, in some crazy way, equating my pain with his, and I think our grief unites us in some macabre bond.

Perhaps I'm insane, but I feel there is a symmetry here that I can almost touch. I want him to speak to me, to look into my eyes and for me to be able to comfort him and for him to comfort me. We are two sides of the same coin.

I leave him where he is, alone in his sadness. I carry my own grief up the deck and away from him. I'm an idiot for thinking he can give me anything.

It's a long voyage ahead.


1925-1928: France and England


There are many pleasures in life, but none compare to the few hours of euphoria brought on by the injection of the morphine-based drug heroin. As soon as I thought clearly again, I knew that I wanted, no — I *needed* to feel that way all the time. The next morning, as Orla and her brother were preparing to depart, I asked him where he had gotten the gift he had shared with us. He told me where I could procure more, but gave me a word of warning.

"Be careful, Helen," he said.

I laughed in response.

Once I secured a source of this drug, life in France became fluid and less volatile. I missed Orla deeply, but having heroin allowed me to accept life without her. I isolated myself. I wrote all the time. I laid on the beach and floated in my mind. I stopped thinking of my past so much. I was happy.

I had stopped thinking about men. So, of course, I met one — a painter by the name of Stuart Edmonds. Edmonds was the opposite of Ferguson in almost every way. He was creative, funny, and oftentimes deeply sensitive. But like Ferguson, he was an alcoholic; however, where Ferguson was angry and violent, Edmonds was maudlin and self-hating. I spent the next decade with him.

I remember the first time I saw him — he was laughing as he tipped a champagne glass to his lips. He was smartly dressed in a wool suit that matched the contours of his tall and fit frame. I endeavored to make him mine. I was still desperately lonely, and conversations with Edmonds stimulated me. I wanted someone to love me, to sympathize with me, to *know* me. I developed a hold on him by impressing him intellectually. We liked much of the same things; we shared a taste in art and literature of the avant-garde; surrealism and modernism were in vogue, and wild feats of the imagination were celebrated. Edmonds and I wanted to be celebrated too.

I had finished my manuscript and sent it to a publisher I knew in London. He loved it and wanted to publish it. I had high hopes of living a life of success and recognition. Don't all artists? I fantasized about having an income where I could support myself and not be dependent on my mother. My career was finally a reality.

Edmonds broke France's hold on me, and I moved back to England to be with him. He was married but pledged his love to me. However, his family was strictly Catholic, and a divorce from his wife seemed impossible.

Sadly, he was dependent on his father's support. Once his father found out he was gallivanting with a fallen woman such as myself, his father's judgment became a living part of our relationship. I realize now that spice helped distract from things that would have otherwise eroded our romance. As the newness of our love wore off, I noticed things about Edmonds that I didn't like, such as his incessant drinking, his jealousies, and when my book was published, his envy and feelings of inadequacy. Of course, I had my own shortcomings — who doesn't? — but I was forgiving of mine.

Once my book was published, I received a small stipend; not as much as I would have liked, but it helped. I celebrated that critics responded favorably to my work and took up my pen with more purpose. As my success grew, things started to shift between Edmonds and myself. He painted prodigiously; however, no one was interested in his work. He would belittle my success to compensate for his failures. Looking back, I agree with his critics — he was not talented. I was only pretending. Even if he had it, talent isn't enough — you need something *else,* some holy fire that burns like a fierce star that will not be ignored. Edmonds did not have that. We all knew it.

I continued to believe in him, despite his frustration with my success. The years passed, and his paintings never caught anyone's eye — not the eyes that mattered, anyway. He drank more to numb the pain of his failure, and his once fit body became round and flabby. I found myself looking at him with disgust.

Despite our waning love affair, I became pregnant again. While I had little interest in having another child, Edmonds was excited. He already had children with his wife, but he claimed they were not the product of true love — like ours would be. Desperate to make him happy, I thought having his baby would be the answer to all his grief. The path I took had been shared by many women trying to please the men they loved.

Once Edmonds' family found out I was pregnant, they allowed him to divorce his wife. The church, of course, was swayed with a mighty donation from Edmonds' father. We were hastily married and waited for the child to arrive.


1941: Onboard *The Wanderer*


Another night of lousy sleep left me restless. Though the ship rocks me like a baby in my cabin, I cannot take that final step into proper rest. Alcohol doesn't help, and I refuse the comforts of heroin. My mind races in the dark.

The next morning the sky is gray again, and the air is cold. After the tasteless breakfast, I maneuver myself over the undulating deck to the bar, where I find Novak having his after-work drink.

"You promised," I tell him, grinning.

"I did," he says, finishing his drink. "Follow me."

Inside his cabin, there is a small berth neatly made with hospital corners. A small desk and chair and a tiny wardrobe fills the rest of the room. The smell of men's sweat permeated the small room. On his desk sit two portraits of women.

"Who is this?" I ask, pointing to the frame on the left.

"My wife."

I'm surprised. Perhaps I was wrong in thinking him to be queer.

"Do you miss her?"

"A little," he admits.

"Do you have any children?"

"A daughter. I miss her more."

I pick up the other picture. "And who is this?"

"My sister."

"Are you close?"

"We were very close."

His words sink into my head.

"'Were'?"

"She passed away."

"I'm sorry," I say. "What happened?"

Novak rubs his cheek absently. "She got an infection from a venereal disease her husband gave her. He couldn't keep his hands off the prostitutes."

"And what happened to him?"

Novak draws a breath and sighs. "I killed him."

Shock rings through me. Gruesome images flash in my head — Novak choking another man, or stabbing him. Perhaps shooting him. Once the shock abates, I feel forgiveness for Novak.

"You loved her very much," I observe.

"Completely."

"And that is why you hide on the seas? Can you not return?"

"No," says Novak, emphatically. "I cannot return."

"And your wife and child?"

"I have dishonored them. They do not miss me."

I watch him for a moment, trying to measure his tragedy. As Yeats sang, '*there is more sorrow in the world than we can understand.*'

"Do you want to kiss me?" I ask.

He stares into my eyes.

"I like men," he says.

I nod in acceptance. It isn't so strange for him to have a wife and child. Plenty of homosexual men do.

"I understand," I say, trying to hide my disappointment. "Why did you invite me here, then?"

"I thought you needed a friend," he says.

"I do," I say. "Need a friend."

My eyes fall on his small berth.

"Do you want to lie down with me?" I ask.

"But…" he says. "I told you…"

"We could just hold each other. Be the comfort we are both in need of."

I see the darkness in his eyes giving way to light.

"Okay," he says.

"Nothing will happen," I promise. "We will be like innocent babes."

I lie next to him on the bed, enjoying the warmth of his body. Once we are lying together, I realize how much I missed the touch of another human being. Novak is on his back, and I'm curled on my side, my arm lightly across his chest. I bury my face in the nape of his neck.

"Do you like this?" I whisper.

"Yes."

He speaks honestly. Perhaps I am not the only one who misses human touch.

Novak is silent for a moment. I feel he wants to express something difficult for him.

"My sister and I used to sleep like this when we were children," he tells me. "My father was always at sea, and my mother was a drunkard. We hid from her. Even as we got older, and I was no longer a boy, and she was no longer a girl…"

"Because she knew you would never hurt her."

"Yes."

"And you will not hurt me?"

"No! I will not."

I exhale into his skin. I can feel his heart pulse.

I am perfectly happy.

I gave birth to a girl. I was not allowed to hold her pale, limp body for long. She did not live for more than a few days. Of course, we can blame fate and fortune, but I knew it was due to my addiction. The doctors showed their judgment with their critical faces. Edmonds had little sympathy for me as well.

I was surprised by my grief. Death is always sad, I suppose. I do wonder what would have become of my daughter. I loved her in a way that I could never love my son — despite her short life.

As painful and confusing as the loss was, I felt relief as the days and weeks passed. I wasn't meant to be a mother. I was a terrible mother to the son I already had. I had been a fool to think a child could be a salvation for Edmonds and me.

Edmonds cracked. He took his pain out on me and became angry. He drank more. He resented me and outwardly blamed me for our daughter's death. We fought — violently. Everything that was ever good between us decayed. Our marriage became a trap for both of us. But when I spoke of divorce, he became belligerent.

"And disappoint my family even more?" He thundered.

I was getting older but still considered myself a young woman. I felt strangled by Edmonds, pressed down. I found it hard to remember the good times we had. I was unhappy — no, anguished, suffering, tortured.

I knew I had loved him once. Sometimes I had been feverish with him. But was that love? Isn't love supposed to be something beyond imagination?

I felt like I was on a stopped conveyor belt, with the future's fangs before me — a life pinned to Edmonds. And other times, the whole world felt like a vast, rolling wilderness of wicked trees and hidden, bloodthirsty beasts. I was just a girl. But it was no fairytale, and no knight was coming to save me.

Desperate to escape, I tried to kill myself again, this time with pills. I failed. I was committed to an asylum, and my mother was informed of my addiction. It was carelessness on my part, as I had not registered with the government as a morphine addict, and had infections due to the use of dirty needles.

My mother was irritated that she still had to look after me at my age.

"When you are not killing yourself with dramatics, you are killing yourself with that poison!" She angrily exclaimed when she visited me.

"The dangers of heroin are greatly exaggerated," I told her venomously.

"You've been committed! How is that an exaggeration!"

I had never seen her so upset.

When Edmonds' father found out I had been committed to an asylum, it was the last straw. He gave Edmonds an ultimatum — leave me or be cut off financially.

Edmonds did not take much time to make a decision. I was not as valuable to him as his father's money. The divorce was set in motion.

Once again, I was adrift.

I lie with Novak for a long time. We fall asleep soundly until his shift. When we say goodbye, I kiss him tenderly on the cheek. There is a newfound peace in his eyes, and, I think, in my heart.

I return to my cabin to collect my thoughts. I feel inspired. I write. I write about a sailor who left everything he knows for a lonely life on the sea. The words flow with only the slightest intervention on my part. Sometimes the white page is as opaque and unfathomable as the sea. But not today; today it is as clear as a bright sunny sky.

When evening comes, I go to sleep.

I awake elated the next morning and make my way upstairs to the dining hall. For the first time during my trip, the food tastes good. Afterwards, I head to the bar. Novak is sitting at his usual place, having his after-work drink. I smile at him, but his eyes are cloaked; there is a weight to them.

I try to lighten the mood by cheekily asking if he wants to go back to his cabin. He declines.

"Why?" I ask.

"Because…" he speaks. "I don't think it's right."

"Why not?"

"Because… I cannot be what you want."

My heart tumbles. "And what do you think I want?"

"A man who will never hurt you." He takes a sip of his drink. "And you can never be what I want. You can never be my sister."

I look down at my shoes. "I suppose not."

I take a sip from my drink, not knowing what to say.

Desperate to change the subject he says, "Hey, your name, Kavan. It's Czech, isn't it?"

"I made it up," I tell him. "It's not my real name."

Novak frowns. "And what is your real name?"

I take a moment to respond. "It was Helen Woods."

"Was? Why did you change it?"

"Because I killed someone too," I say at last.

"Who?"

"The woman I used to be. I killed her. At least I thought I had. I thought I was different, my life was different. But nothing's changed; I can't escape my past."

"I understand," he says. "I can't escape mine either."

We drink together for another half hour, and then Novak excuses himself to get some sleep. This time he kisses *me* on the cheek. I can tell it's over. It was just an illusion. Novak is right; it wouldn't work between us. I was fooling myself.

I feel miserable; achingly alone and lonely. So…lost.

There's only one way to calm my nerves. I go back to my cabin and open my luggage, pulling out the leather case that holds my kit. I sit at the table, unlatch the strap, and pull out the syringe and my little bottle of white powder.

My dearest.

I place the bottle on top of the typewriter's keys and stare at it for a long time.

I was in the asylum for six months. You don't know what freedom is until you've been deprived of it.

When I left the asylum, I had a Damascus moment. During my *incarceration*, I worked on an autobiographical novel portraying my relationship with Edmonds, and invented a character based on myself. I named her Anna Kavan. All of my work was loosely autobiographical, though not entirely true — not in terms of the facts — there was a higher truth I was after, that could only be found in fiction.

The inspiration for the name "Anna Kavan" had popped into my head one day in the asylum. I realized, once I was free, that I *was* Anna Kavan, and she was me. The difference between reality and fiction was negligible. Anna Kavan wasn't real, but she was true — the true version of me.

I realized that as close as we become to others during our lives, we are all trapped, isolated, in our individual stories that begin with our births and end with our deaths. Our worlds are entirely subjective; we are imprisoned in our minds and bodies, and can only speculate on the world outside of ourselves. There is no difference between a character in a book and a person in life. Both are illusory and in the end, both ultimately intangible and transient.

I desperately wanted to be someone else, rewrite a new ending for myself. But how could I when I didn't even know who I was? I wasn't Helen Woods, or Helen Ferguson, or Helen Edmonds. I was fiction. I was Anna Kavan.

I legally changed my name. Soon enough, Anna Kavan had a new life and traveled the world — meeting new men.

There was a gentleman who caught my eye. He was a good man, perhaps the best I ever met. He came from Old Money, and he was handsome, with inquisitive blue eyes, and he always smelled delightful. He believed that war was coming, and he had no intention of fighting in it, so we escaped to Bali, where he owned a house on the beach. It was a beautiful and warm place to escape to. We spent our days baking in the sun, and at night we danced.

Still, sometimes I would find myself morose. When we sat on the beach watching the ocean, we would talk and laugh, but an incredible sense of loneliness would strike me. It took time, but I managed to procure heroin locally and started using again to feel happy. Drugs can be found anywhere, especially by people with money and determination.

This nice man; this good man; this *best* man, disapproved.

I was getting older. My skin sagged, and my beauty was fading. In a way, I didn't mind, as it freed me from the unwanted attention of men. At the same time, I felt a loss. Being beautiful had been part of my identity, and it was diminishing. Aches and mysterious pains lingered in my body. My face developed lines that could not be washed away or hidden by makeup.

My mind stayed constant. It was the one thing I could not escape. I had accumulated wisdom in age; however, it didn't help. Every night, I battled with sleep. Every day the hours lumbered. What had seemed a paradise became Hell.

My partner sensed I was unhappy. I became less attentive. While understanding at first, he grew discouraged by my temperament. Our love, if it had ever existed beyond faint traces, dissolved.

He asked me to leave.

I booked passage on a ship. On our last night together, he cooked me dinner, and I drank too much wine. He thought we could remain friends.

"Maybe you'll find what you're looking for out there," he said.

"How can you be so sure?"

"I'm hopeful. The problem, Anna, is you are not."

I scoffed. "You sound like my psychoanalyst."

"That doesn't mean I'm wrong."

I thought for a moment, letting his words sink in.

"I didn't plan to make you miserable," I told him at last. "I know I am… unwell. But maybe I could love you."

"But you don't love yourself, Anna."

"What is there to love?" I asked flippantly.

"I wonder that myself," he answered. Even the nicest men are not nice sometimes.

"You didn't have to say that," I said softly.

"I'm sorry," he told me. "I didn't mean to hurt you. But you're going to have to figure this out on your own. I tried. No one can help you — but you."

He was right, and I knew it. He *was* a nice man. He didn't mean to hurt me. But he couldn't help me. We both knew it.

The next day, I said goodbye to him and left for the sea.

The ship was named *The Wanderer.*


<u>1941: Onboard *The Wanderer*</u>


Feeling a little better, and a little disappointed in myself, I make my way up to the deck. It is gray and drizzling, but there are blue lakes of sky amidst the clouds, and I wonder if the sun might yet come out. The sea extends forever around the ship; it's hard to believe there is such a thing as land.

My curiosity encourages me to walk to the stern of the ship. I watch the old gentleman sitting alone in his deck chair, staring blankly out to sea. I watch him for a while. He is motionless; however, the wind makes his hair and the tails of his coat flutter. The world is silent except for the engine's humming sound and the pattering of drizzle on the deck.

I casually approach him. Once again, he does not acknowledge me. I say nothing. Instead, I drag a chair over and sit next to him, close enough to touch. My face and hair are wet with the rain.

I speak —

"My father … threw himself off the bow of a steamer when I was fourteen. No one knows why. From that moment, he was gone forever."

The man slowly turns to me, and his blue eyes lift to meet mine, something spreading in them. He looks at his shoes.

"My daughter," he says. "She was so…" he grapples for the word, "lost."

I see his hand trembling. I imagine reaching out and taking it in my own. I wonder if he would squeeze it back. Then *something* would happen.

But it's just a fantasy. Instead, there is only the sea that carried us here.

# The Last Wish of Gustave Flaubert

Gustave sighed as he looked up from his book to catch sight of his favorite prostitute, Éliane, washing at the basin in the corner of the room. Women. Poor creatures. Why were they cursed to be considered the lesser sex when there was nothing "lesser" about them? They seemed fated to always be secondary—a man had his liberty—but a woman's plight was wholly different.

Gustave continued to stare. What had led Éliane here? He knew her deceased parents had been drunkards, but had she been doomed simply because of her sex? He considered her dreams—had she ever had any? The human capacity for romantic delusions was boundless; dreams sustain and strangle us at once. However, a woman's unfulfilled dreams seemed more tragic to him than the vain pursuits of men.

Letting out another sigh, Gustave returned to his book, written by Lord Byron. A laugh trembled through him as he read a passage that tickled him —

*"Truth is always strange, stranger than fiction."*

"Yes, my Lord Byron," he said under his breath. "But fiction is *truer* than truth!"

Éliane turned her head. "Did you say something?"

Gustave cleared his throat. "No, no, my sweetheart, I am just reading."

"Ah." Éliane smiled, returning to her ritual.

Fiction was truer than truth. Gustave decided immediately this was impossibly correct. He told himself to write down this diamond of wisdom, or at least remember it. But he would not.

Éliane finished and returned to the bed.

Her voice was always soft. "Are you staying over tonight, my sweetheart?"

"Yes, if you don't mind," Gustave replied. "It is a long walk back home, and it is quite dark. Will it, ah, cost me anything?"

"Only if you want another go," she told him. "Sleeping is free. Besides, I like a warm body to lay next to at night."

He doubted he would want 'another go'; she had ridden him to his completion, as often happened these days. He lacked the stamina to do the work himself. He was in ill health; however, the sexual desire in him was as ravenous as ever.

Éliane crawled into the bed. Gustave lifted his arm as she laid her head on his chest and wrapped her leg across his crotch. He felt her warm breath on his skin.

Women. Glorious!

But at what cost?

*

The following day Gustave awoke, said goodbye to Éliane, and started his walk back to his home in the hamlet of Croisset, France. He had lived there most of his life, abhorring the city of Paris — he was more content with a slower pace of life, cleaner air, and a greener environment. Being fifty-eight, the exercise was good for him. However, he knew his feet and back would ache terribly by the time he arrived home.

It was May, spring was in the air, and the morning was warm and filled with golden light. The year was 1880.

Gustave Flaubert was one of the most famous writers in France. His first novel, *Madame Bovary*, created quite a stir when it hd been published. His depiction of a scandalous woman led the government to put him on trial for immorality, inadvertently giving him additional fame, resulting in the sales of more copies of his book.

Who were the bourgeoisie to judge *him*?

He, of course, was acquitted.

Despite his success as an author, Gustave's finances were not good, and he was suffering from loneliness. His beloved Mother, whom he had lived with for most of his life, had passed away eight years ago. Gustave had not fully recovered from the loss. He missed her dearly.

As Gustave made his way down the winding road towards his home, he thought about the women who had passed through his life and what they meant to him. He undoubtedly had loved them all, some just a little, and some quite a lot. In public, Gustave gave the impression of being notoriously unsentimental; but… inside his heart, he was quite a different person. It was his own ego that prevented him from succumbing to romantic passions in public. That did not mean he did not partake in them privately.

Gustave tried to remember all the prostitutes that he had loved for only an evening. He was reminded of his contemplations from the night before — had they only been born men, many of these women's hardships would not exist. Women were allowed so few opportunities in this day and age, so little freedom, trapped in domesticity, dependent on men. As Gustave was not a man of faith, he found only one thing to blame for this treachery on the fairer sex — society. Society was at fault for the confines placed on women. Tradition, law, habit, and laziness had rendered the female sex into nothing more than slavery.

Women's servitude was invented by men. It was not part of the natural order. In the wild, female mammals were more than self-sufficient. They lived on their own, raised their young singlehandedly. Males, in many cases, were only needed for the conception of future offspring.

Arguably, men were physically stronger, but Gustave knew plenty of women whose hearts were more courageous than any man he had met. That emotional strength was deeply undervalued because to recognize it would mean women must be given more power.

Gustave continued his journey home. His breath became labored. The walk was slow and arduous. It allowed him time to think about the more profound things in life. As it often did, Gustave's mind turned to his poor protagonist, Emma Bovary, whom was also caught up in the unfairness of the female plight. She had been as trapped as many other women in her time, and she paid for it dearly. Critics claimed Gustave had been deriding romantic delusions when he wrote *Madame Bovary*; he was criticized for the black liquid that came out of her throat when she was dead. These critics didn't understand his purpose.

Emma Bovary simply wanted to escape the mundanity of her father's dreary farm, thinking marriage was a way to a new life — foolish girl. Instead, she found herself with a hapless husband, the drudgery of domesticity, and the eternal misery of an unhappy marriage. Is it any wonder she destroyed herself with sexual liaisons and succumbed to a mad hedonism, spiraling into debt and ruin?

She imagined suicide would be a romantic escape.

Instead, it was only the pitiful climax of her suffering.

*

Gustave returned to his empty house exhausted. His housekeeper was scheduled to show up in the afternoon, but for now, it was too quiet. He felt an overwhelming sense of loneliness, so he decided to have some bread and wine and peruse a journal he recently purchased in Paris. Sitting under a tree in the garden, he enjoyed the spring air and slowly caught his breath. How had he gotten so old?

As he made his way through the magazine, he was caught off guard — there was an article written about him and his illustrious novel *Madame Bovary*. He gritted his teeth as he found the article criticized both his person, and his work. The last paragraph read —

> *The idea that Flaubert is an author who will transcend his time is preposterous — his "fame," if that is what you want to call it, will not live past his increasingly inevitable death. The crass lack of sentiment in his books is a product of our ill time, and such a style will be mercifully forgotten as the years pass. At best, Flaubert is nothing but a scandal that has passed like a gastronomical knot.*

Gustave's heart deflated and sank. He never paid much attention to the critics, but this put a dagger directly into his heart, attacking the center of his vanity — his dream of immortality. His every desire was to be remembered for hundreds, if not thousands of years through his prose. Why shouldn't he be spoken of in the same breath as Homer and Shakespeare? If this critic couldn't see the generosity in his work, perhaps no one could. Now, as old age attacked and death approached, he felt it was all for naught. How would he be remembered if no one understood him?

Never one to ignore coincidence, Gustave considered the portent of finding this article when his thoughts strayed over the very same subject repeatedly in the morning hours. He had tried to be invisible in the text, offering no commentary, no opinions, no judgments so that the story could be objective. He realized now that his biases had been so invisible that readers had misunderstood him completely — they finished the book, thinking he condemned Emma for her thirst for life. Was she not human? He never would have spent so much time and labor writing about a person he hated.

The truth was, he loved Emma.

They were one and the same.

Gustave wondered — was it too late to redeem his heroine? Or was she bound to be forever cast as one of the villains of literature? That certainly had not been his intention. An idea tossed in his head — he could write a follow-up novel. It seemed a near impossibility — she was dead — but he needed to do something.

His mind raced. What if… what if he wrote of Emma's early years before she married — when her young and innocent ideals of the world were not yet destroyed? When her romantic hopes were luminescent and beautiful? It could be a pure *jour dans la vie*, a "day in the life" where the mundane moments would be sacraments. She could be redeemed.

Yes, he thought. This he could do, and he would call it…a "prequel."

*

Gustave immediately took up ink and paper. It could not be a long piece of work, perhaps a novella. He was so exhausted these days and unsure of his writing capabilities. But self-doubt had no place in this project, the obstacles didn't matter — he must do it for his Emma.

Starting a piece of work was always the biggest challenge for Gustave. Once he finalized the first sentence, the rest seemed to write itself, but that first sentence was his mountain to climb. He licked his lips and tried to focus. He thought of Emma, lying on her back in the grass, looking up at the blue sky, wishing that her life was full of adventure, and losing herself in one of her romantic novels. Yes, that is how it would start, he thought, it would be mid-morning, springtime, and she would be innocently happy —

> *It was at Monsieur Rouault's farm, near Tôtes, in May. Spring had blossomed; the air was sweet, and it had rained lightly the night before. Monsieur Rouault's daughter Emma lay upon the grass, the damp earth soaking through the back of her linen dress as she stared enrapt at the traces of clouds like smudges of flour on the pale sapphire sky.*

By late afternoon Gustave had written the opening paragraphs and was plagued by exhaustion. When his housekeeper, Madame Thibeau, arrived, he barely noticed her presence. She made him a simple dinner of chicken cutlets and green beans. The smell of the food made him acknowledge his hunger. He sucked the chicken and beans into his mouth happily before returning to his story.

Madame Thibeau was thin, with twig-like wrists. Despite her small stature, she was a hard worker and cleaned his house as if she was a staff of three. She was uneducated and grew up on a poor farm, but she knew how to work. Gustave paid her handsomely.

"What are you working on?" she asked after beating the dust from a rug.

Gustave could see droplets of sweat drip from her brow. He was annoyed that someone with her lack of education could possibly presume to understand his work.

"Oh," he said, "just a little nothing, like all art." She didn't seem to be someone who enjoyed literature.

Madame Thibeau smirked, cursing under her breath. Gustave felt immediate guilt for treating her with disrespect and spoke anew.

"I am correcting a past mistake in some of my earlier work," he announced. "So, posterity will forgive my young foolishness."

"Ah, we are all fools when we are young," his housekeeper opined.

"That may be true," he agreed. "But I must correct myself before it's too late. My immortality is at stake. It is hard to explain oneself posthumously."

"Immortality?" she repeated. "There is no such thing."

"People are going to remember me," said Gustave. "That's enough."

She shrugged. "How are you feeling?" she asked.

"Terribly!" he admitted.

She recommended a salve for his joints and a tea for his throat. He scoffed at both.

"I'm going back to work," he told her.

"I'll clean up," Madame Thibeau replied, as if granting him permission to be excused.

Gustave went back to his study and lit an oil lamp. Sitting his large, fat body at the desk, he felt bloated and lethargic after his dinner. Despite these ailments, he pressed on, taking more paper and ink to continue with his work. After a short while, he took the page to his window and read out loud in a sonorous voice, testing the beauty of the prose, or lack thereof. It sounded decent — but decent wasn't good enough. If he wanted to be remembered forever, he must do better.

The work went notoriously slow. Only the right words would do in all situations, and they were not easy to find. Gustave painfully agonized over every sentence, and his work slowed as the sun set. By the time the sun fully went down, he was barely writing half-sentences. He was tripping over each phrase, feeling bogged down by the lack of accuracy each sentence afforded him.

He compromised with himself — it would have to be only a short story. A novella would surely kill him. As a short story, it would be efficient beyond compare, almost rudimentary. It must redeem him. It must redeem Emma.

Lack of inspiration forced him to take a break. He went out back beneath the night sky. Feeling alone with the cosmos, he yelled out to the river Seine that flowed in the back of his property.

"None of them understand me! And now I must correct them! Don't you understand I was critical of the bourgeoisie, not defending them! Bastards!" Defeat emphasized every word.

Feeling he had said his piece to the universe, Gustave returned to his desk and quickly fell asleep sitting upright in his chair.

*

Gustave awoke the next day having dreamt of a cow in a meadow, grazing on the land. Inspiration hit, as it often did after a vivid dream. He knew Emma would have a favorite cow on her father's farm that she would milk and take care of; it would be named… Clotilde. Emma could walk in the fields and speak to Clotilde, and the cow would be her closest friend and confidante, privy to all her deepest secrets and fantasies.

Needing experience and inspiration for his story, Gustave decided to visit the farmer whose property neighbored his own. He walked down through the grass, soaking his boots in the moisture from the dew. He found his neighbor, Monsieur Ouellet, fixing a piece of fence.

"I say, my good man," Gustave began. "I don't suppose you'd teach me how to milk one of your cows? It is for a story I'm writing."

"Well, that is quite the request, Monsieur Flaubert. It is not as easy as you would think," Ouellet chuckled. He had bushy blond eyebrows and a red face. His arms were covered in copper-colored hair, and he had callused hands.

"So be it," said Gustave. "You will be helping me greatly."

The farmer led Gustave to his barn where the cows mooed from being confined. Gustave inhaled the sharp smell of manure and the acrid odor of the cows. Fighting the desire to retch, he imagined Emma enjoying the scent as she approached her beloved animal.

Ouellet showed him how to place his hand gently but firmly on the cow's teat and squeeze in a downward motion until the milk released. It took greater pressure than Gustave imagined. In his head, he thought that the cow's teat was "as soft as an infant's shoulders" — a simile he would use in his story. Afterwards, Monsieur Ouellet poured the milk in a cup and Gustave drank it, imagining the creamy flavor dancing on Emma's tongue. The liquid was thick and wet his mustache; it was warm and sweet; he swallowed happily. A drop spilled from his mouth and trickled down his neck; he fantasized Emma wiping it from herself with her sleeve.

Gustave thanked Ouellet and hurried back home, eager to write. But all his imaginings and imagery from before failed him. After half an hour, he was crippled by his extreme exhaustion. He struggled to remember his experiences at the farm and was greeted by a blistering headache. He feared he might not finish the story. The empty pages taunted him like an impenetrable fortress.

In a futile attempt to ignore his exhaustion, Gustave pushed on through the morning, only to find himself entirely spent by noon, with nothing but nonsense written on the paper. He only had completed two pages — not enough. He went into the kitchen and had some sardines, a jar of which, Madame Thibeau, as always, had cooling in a bowl of water. He washed them down with a glass of wine, savoring the conflicting tastes.

His arm ached. He scolded himself for caring. In his youth, he would write for sixteen hours a day and not worry about the cramps that would come. Surely, he could conjure some semblance of that productivity. How had he gotten *so* old?

Somehow, he went from complaining in his head about his arm to awaking suddenly in his chair. He had fallen asleep! What wasted time! He read his measly pages aloud. They sounded adequate, but adequate was not enough. He was unsure how many pages it would take to redeem Emma in the eyes of his audience. Ten? Twenty? More? He could barely imagine.

Madame Thibeau showed up later that day and heated a stew she had made at her home. He ate it hungrily. She inquired once again about his writing.

"It goes," he replied. "I am old."

"We are both old," she told him.

"But your work ends when the sun sets," he told her.

"Does it?" she asked. "I never thought of it that way."

They were silent for a moment. Gustave sighed as an idea struck him.

"Madame," he said, "What did you dream of when you were a girl?"

Madame Thibeau thought for a moment, and light briefly flashed across her face. She frowned. "Why speak of such things?" She replied. "It is nonsense."

"It is not nonsense!" He protested. "It is the key!"

"To doors that should not be opened," she countered.

"Please," he said. "I'm only trying to understand the female heart."

She pressed her hand to her chest and closed her eyes. "I wanted to sail the seas."

"Oh?"

Madame Thibeau opened her eyes and stared out the window.

"I had an older cousin who was a sailor. When he visited, he told me of his life on the sea. It filled me with longing — I wanted to float on a ship on the ocean, surrounded by endless shimmering water, the whole world beckoning for me to explore and discover."

Gustave cleared his throat. "That is beautiful," he told her.

She sighed. "I have never sailed on the ocean."

"It is not too late…"

"No," she said sadly. "It is."

"Redemption is possible," he argued, though he realized he was mostly trying to convince himself. "That is why I am writing now."

"What does it matter?" She asked. "Enjoy life."

"But to enjoy life, I must finish this, I must!" he said. "It is imperative for posterity's view of me!" Gustave was plagued by vanity. So be it, he thought. He wanted his name and work to live on forever.

He shooed Madame Thibeau out of the house and went back to work. The day was growing late. Having eaten and rested, he found a new wind. He returned to his place in the story —

> *Emma's father headed to town, and Emma decided to sneak into his bedroom to get a sense of who her deceased Mother was, and why her father loved her so. She pressed open the door to her father's room like it was an imperial gate, gently stepping inside to a forbidden palace. The wide bed sat foremost in the room, with two wardrobes, a chest, and a small desk by the window. Cool gray light slithered through the glass. She looked about curiously, hoping for some private revelation. Her eyes fell to her Mother's wardrobe, made of stained oak. Gently pulling open one side, Emma found it untouched since her Mother's death — inside were dresses and skirts, soft fabrics speaking of many things. Emma sniffed the material, hoping to ignite a plentitude of memories, but smelled nothing she recognized. She touched the silk scarves and felt empty. Her eyes trailed to the bottom of the armoire, where two pairs of her Mother's shoes sat; mud was still caked on the toes of one pair.*

Gustave stopped. He realized Emma hadn't only inherited her Mother's shoe size — but also her lack of opportunities as a woman. He contemplated Emma's Mother. He was intrigued by the coldness of the relationship. Indeed, she abandoned her daughter in death. Perhaps Emma lost her Mother before that. What had Emma's Mother's dreams been?

Gustave raised himself from his desk. He climbed the stairs so he could get real rest by sleeping in his bed.

"Tomorrow, I will write more than today," he promised himself.

*

When the sun woke him the next morning, Gustave still felt the exhaustion in his body. A cramp plagued his writing wrist. He swore loudly and coughed as pain wracked his lungs. His genitals itched, and he blamed Éliane.

He contemplated Emma's story. Her father would return from town and notice his wife's shoes on Emma's feet. The pain of seeing them out of the wardrobe would tear him in two, and he would strike Emma. Emma would flee out of the house and into the fields. The climax of the story would come when she is caught in a torrential rainstorm, as she soaks up the raindrops and dances in an almost pagan display of transcendence.

Gustav set upon Emma's redemption, trying not to think of the cramp in his wrist. His mind struggled to find words he knew his younger self would have had no trouble with. The ending waited like a perfect jewel of light. Gustave was just fearful of the journey to get there.

By sunset, he reached five and a half pages. The soreness of his wrist travelled up to his shoulder, making it difficult for him to raise his arm higher than his waist. The pain left him breathless. When Madame Thibeau arrived, in a plea of desperation, he asked her if she knew how to read and write.

"A little," she responded. "I studied with an uncle who was a priest in my girlhood."

"Good!" he praised. He set up the paper, his favorite crystal frog inkwell, and a multitude of goose quills on the table. Leading her by the arm, he sat her down and instructed her that he would dictate his work, and she would write it down.

"What?" she asked, confused.

"My dear," he explained. "My wrist is injured. I must finish this story. You must help me."

She appeared bashful. "But Monsieur Flaubert, I only know a little!"

"A little will have to be a lot today," he told her.

Gustave began dictating, and she made simple strokes across the paper. When he checked her work, he was disappointed. "But you must write faster. You have missed half of my words."

"I am writing fast!" she protested.

"Faster!" he scolded.

Gustave continued dictating, trying to remember what he planned in his head that day.

"My wrist hurts now too," she complained.

"You've only begun!" he argued. After a stern look, Madame Thibeau returned to the pages.

He paused to consider words and phrases and continued, often checking her work. He grudgingly slowed down and repeated himself constantly to allow her to catch up.

"Monsieur!" Madame Thibeau pleaded, rubbing her wrist and dropping the quill. She pushed her chair away from the table in a huff.

"I am sorry, Monsieur Flaubert, but I cannot do it!"

"Please, you must!" he shouted.

"I have my own work. I'm going to cook dinner now. I cannot write for you."

"Oh, forget dinner!"

"Monsieur, I'm sorry, I don't know these words and I cannot help. Please, release me from this endeavor."

Gustave sighed. There was no use arguing with her. She barely produced more than he could do himself. Her lack of education made her unable to complete the task.

"Fine," he growled, withdrawing to his office, taking her pages with him.

*

Gustave spent the next day in bed, depressed, the story fluttering throughout his mind. Oily despair dripped in the caverns of his heart and stomach. What if this was it? He might already be at death's door, with no time left to finish his masterpiece. The doctor had instructed him a week ago to rest for the sake of his life. He realized he might never finish this work. Gustave anguished over it all being a waste of time, fretting he would be forgotten as the years passed by, that his work would mean nothing, that no one would ever understand him.

Gustave begged his wrist to cooperate and improve, massaging it with the fingers of his other hand until a cramp set in in *that* wrist. He cursed as the sunlight came through the windows indicating that the day had aged and he had written little. He reached over to his night table and picked up the pages he had completed. They felt good in his fingers.

He took a tincture of laudanum for the pain. He felt his body go numb. How had he gotten so old? How much longer would death wait?

He panicked that he might never reach Emma's beautiful rainstorm, where her hair and dress would be soaked, and her face would glisten as the water cleansed her of all sin and fear.

The day waned. When Madame Thibeau showed up to prepare him dinner, he greeted her with a sullen face and sunken shoulders. She was nervous about entering the house as he had not adequately forgiven her for being unable to help with his story the night before. He spitefully claimed he was not hungry for her dinner.

Madame Thibeau saw that he was broken and took pity on him.

"What is wrong, Monsieur? Why are you making yourself ill with this?" she asked.

"I cannot finish it!" he told her.

"That is rubbish," she said.

"You do not know how I feel," he muttered.

"It will pass. It does not need to ail you so," Madame told him. She went to the kitchen.

He sat in his yard, gazing at the Seine as she cooked. Gustave realized it all came to this — failure. All his work was meaningless. He was disposable, and he had wasted his life on a false idea. His struggles for the unique, right word — nonsense. Nothing mattered.

Madame Thibeau called him in for dinner. He cut and poked at the roasted chicken. It tasted like dirt in his mouth. She placed her hand on his shoulder and pleaded with him to eat. He almost collapsed in depression.

As she left him that night, she gazed at him like one would a dying puppy. But she said nothing. He listened as she closed the door behind her.

Despite the warm air, Gustave felt damp to his bones. Madame Thibeau had constructed a fire before she left for the evening, and Gustave sat next to it as the inky dusk came through the windows. He placed his feet close to flames, letting the fire warm his extremities. He laid back in his chair and breathed deeply, trying to force calm into his bloodstream.

Gustave took the pages he had written and held them close to his chest. They were sacred. This was the best he could do. And it wasn't enough.

What would they say when they found this aborted work? They would pity him — the worst punishment of all! Posterity would analyze it and find that in his last moments, he had become a sentimental old fool. Having an incomplete manuscript was worse than no manuscript at all. It proved that he was *actually* worthy of their criticism.

No. No. Gustave would not allow it. He would rather they never found it than have it torn apart in their rotten teeth.

Gustave read over the story one final time, treasuring the feel of the pages in his fingers. They were so beautiful, but so incomplete without the perfect ending. He inhaled their scent.

He leaned forward in his chair towards the fire. His fingers clutched the pages, not wanting to let the story go — but it was too fragile to leave behind. His life's work was unfinished — it would be impossible to finish — and no one would understand him. If there were any other option, he would take it—but there was none.

A tear fell from his eye. He cast the pages into the fire.

He watched as flames licked the corners of his pages. They lit up quickly then crumbled, turning black and to ash.

Emma was gone. Again.

*

Gustave heard the rumble of thunder outside. He went to his back porch and looked up to the darkened sky. Lightning flashed across the blackness. In another moment, the heavens started casting down rain in sheets.

Emma's storm! It was here!

He ran out into it, quickly becoming soaked. He lifted his head back and opened his mouth, drinking the raindrops. The water was fresh, but not cold. He felt the rain penetrate his clothes and coat his skin.

Running across the field, he imagined Emma doing the same, as she lifted the hem of her dress from her Mother's mud-caked shoes. He thought of her long hair slick against her skull and neck, the water dripping down her chin. He could feel her excitement as nature demonstrated its power and beauty.

"I'm alive!" he shouted, thinking of Emma's melodic voice, as he spun around with his arms outstretched. He imagined his every movement a replica of her own. They were one, across time, fiction had become real, truer than truth.

Gustave laughed, exhilarated by Mother Nature. Exhaustion came upon him, he was dizzy, he could hardly breathe, and his chest pounded. He stumbled into the shelter of the house and collapsed into his chair by the fire, dripping wet. He was depleted — but elated. It all made sense suddenly, everything, every moment in his life, and he was glad he had lived in this beautiful and terrible world, happy that he had experienced things as they were.

He listened to the rain beat on the roof. The storm subsided. He watched as the flames of the fire licked the logs sending little sparks into the air. The logs turned to embers. He watched as the embers turned to cinders.

He closed his eyes and dreamt of his Emma, passing away quietly into history.

Matt Snee is a writer, composer, painter, and photographer. He was born in Nebraska and raised in Delaware. He currently lives in Phoenix, Arizona.